Primal Source

A NOVEL

Charles Bensinger

TIMEWINDOW PUBLICATIONS

V 2.0
ISBN: 1505520983
ISBN 13: 9781505520989
Library of Congress Control Number: 2015907946
CreateSpace Independent Publishing Platform
North Charleston, South Carolina

People of the Change

BOOK THREE

"Water is the driving force of nature."
—Leonardo da Vinci

CHAPTER ONE

British Columbia
Canada

The craggy, granite bluff called to her, yet its time-scoured face remained defiantly silent. Ariel Connelly suspected the stony citadel hid more than mere geology within its cold, grey tower.

The Lake Albion Valley was pinched in-between the Columbia and Cascade Mountain Ranges. Roughly 10,000 years ago, nature's icy hand gouged a deep groove in the earth, now filled with a sinuous flow of water. Pastoral fields and orchards lay astride the sixty-mile-long watercourse. In a remote section of this picturesque valley, the curious wall of stone stood still and inscrutable.

Ariel and Debbie Chen sat together as the van climbed a steep, snaking switchback. The two women had been involuntarily transported to the valley to serve as workers in a heavily guarded complex of residences, greenhouses and fields. They were kept busy twelve hours a day, farming and processing food for a cluster of financial elite who resided in mansions that clung to the mountainsides.

Before leaving her compound, Ariel had grabbed a pair of binoculars from an office drawer. Though a forbidden item, she knew the optics would soon prove useful.

As the vehicle made its way up the mountain road, Ariel scanned the front of the van to confirm their handler was distracted conversing with the driver. Ariel lifted the binoculars from her day-pack, just high enough for Debbie to see.

"It's those unmarked eighteen-wheelers on the road across the lake. Must be about one every hour, nighttime too. They seem to disappear into the base of that granite bluff. I hope to get a better view from up here."

The van halted in the parking lot. Their handler for the day, a bulky man with a hard face, gestured for the group of ten to exit the van. His blue company uniform sported a round patch on the left breast. It featured a picture of a green and brown globe with a lightning bolt running diagonally across it. Above the patch read the words: "Globechek Enterprises," and below it in Latin, it read: *Terra absolutum dominium*—absolute Earth domination.

Ariel relished the cool mountain air and the expansive view of the valley. But escape was her focus, as she could not tolerate being anyone's prisoner. The trick was finding the cracks in the system.

At twenty-seven, Ariel had already logged plenty of extraordinary life experiences. Along with a small group of courageous bio-adventurers, she had chosen to modify her genetic code to generate her own internal energy from sunlight, air and water. Thus, her skin glowed with a distinct green hue. This identified Ariel as a human photosynthesizer—*Homo photosynthese*—having abandoned forever her native species, *Homo sapiens*. Taking advantage of assistance from a most unlikely source, Ariel and her cohorts had provided the world with a powerful new energy technology that fundamentally altered the global geopolitical reality. Ariel's psychic skills and remote-viewing capability had assisted her team members to achieve stunning accomplishments in the face of extreme adversity. As a fledgling photosynthesizer, however, she required a daily regime of plant food and regular genetic inoculation. This dependency had rendered her captive to a powerful cabal and their apocalyptic plans.

Ariel fell behind as the group followed their handler into a forest of pines. Slipping away unnoticed, Ariel made her way to a nearby rocky shoulder. As she lifted the binoculars from her pack, she spotted an unmarked eighteen-wheeler on the opposite side of the lake. Tracking the rig with her optics, Ariel observed it entering into a wide entrance tunnel at the base of the mountain just as a second large truck was pulling out. A tangle of excitement, fear, and foreboding spiraled up her spine. She had to know what secrets the mountain was hiding.

CHAPTER TWO

Later that evening

"The entrance is large enough to fit two big rigs side-by-side, coming and going," said Ariel. "Just what are they trying to conceal? Or prepare for?"

Debbie's mind swirled as she tried to make sense of the situation. "Obviously, somebody is spending a ton of money."

"But why? What for?"

"Governments have been building tunnels and underground facilities ever since the Cold War years. 'It's for protection,' they tell us. But from what? Nuclear War? Plagues? Revolution? Climate Change? Or what's sometimes referred to as a 'Total Loss Event.'"

"Maybe all of the above," suggested Ariel. "We do know they call this place a 'refuge enclave.'"

Ariel's gaze shifted as she continued. "When I look into the mountain with my remote viewing, I get fuzzy pictures of rooms and buildings—many, in fact. Seems crazy, but I need to see for myself what's going on. So how do I get in there? Any suggestions? You're the special-ops expert."

Debbie looked away, leaned back in her chair and thought out loud. "*Stowaway*—on one of the small transport trucks."

"How?"

"Those trucks that pick up the fruits and vegetables. They follow the big rigs down the highway. I bet they're going into the mountain as well."

"And I get myself into one of those produce boxes."

"Alone?" Debbie was visibly concerned.

Ariel collected her thoughts. "This is something I just have to do on my own. Besides, I need you to cover for me and tell my story . . . if, for some reason I don't return . . ." Ariel's eyes teared up unexpectedly.

A shadow of loss crossed Debbie's face. Ariel and Debbie were a team. They had previously faced many hazardous challenges together. Now Ariel was going solo and exposing herself to a multitude of unknown dangers.

"You sure?"

Ariel forced herself to reconsider what she had just proposed. Her skin trembled with a chill. "When the inner voice speaks, I listen. It's like that now."

Debbie understood.

The two women spent every available minute discussing the logistics. Finally, it was time. After the workers had left for the day, Ariel and Debbie entered the darkened warehouse and checked the rooms and corridors for stragglers and security cameras. When they determined they were alone, they weighed both a full and an empty box. They calculated the correct fruit-to-person weight ratio so Ariel's container would not attract any special attention. Finding an old, unused freezer, they set up a working area inside and installed a series of panels into the container so it appeared from the outside that the box was filled with produce.

Over the next several days, Ariel kept a close watch on the trucks arriving to transport foodstuffs to the mountain. Before dawn, on the designated morning, the women moved Ariel's container onto the loading dock. Debbie handed Ariel a pack containing food, water, and emergency gear. Debbie looked deeply into Ariel's eyes.

"I'm not happy you're going by yourself. If you get into trouble, send word and I'll come find you."

Ariel's voice broke with emotion. "What you're saying means a lot to me. I've learned so much from you."

Heart pounding with tense anticipation, Ariel climbed into the four-foot by four-foot crate. Several small holes carved in its sides afforded Ariel an exterior view. Interior latches would allow Ariel to exit the box. It seemed like a good plan, and by mid-morning, a forklift placed Ariel's container into the truck along with twenty other identical crates. The truck, with its produce and human cargo now loaded, pulled out of the warehouse and headed toward its mountain destination.

Since her container was strapped onto the outside edge of the pile of boxes, Ariel could observe the roadside flashing by through her viewing holes. As she sat crunched in the tight space, Ariel felt her fear rising. Settling into a calmer state, she closed her eyes and slowed her breathing. Twenty minutes later, the truck abruptly applied its brakes. Peering through the viewing ports, she could see her vehicle was in line behind a large tractor-trailer. Gunning its engine, the big truck moved forward. Ariel's truck pulled up to the guard shack at the entrance to the tunnel. Her driver and the gatekeeper engaged in a muffled conversation. With a lurch, the truck entered the mountainside. Ariel felt her crate shudder as an eighteen-wheeler passed by on the opposite side of the road. There's a lot of traffic here, she said to herself, further increasing her determination to understand just what was going on—and why.

Ariel's view darkened as her truck sped through the tunnel. She repositioned herself for stability and struggled to get her bearings, but all she could see were white concrete walls rushing by. The vehicle slowed and Ariel gasped in astonishment. The tunnel opened up into a vast cavern that contained an entire village—with apartments, retail stores and a small park, complete with trees and green vegetation. Streets were filled with people carrying packages and chatting with others. Ariel craned her head attempting to identify the source of the convincing daylight effect, but her field of view was too limited. As she returned her attention to the village, she observed that a station platform had been constructed against the far wall of the cavern. Next to the station was parked a state-of-the-art, high-speed passenger train. Its gleaming blue and white design accented the futuristic locomotive that stood ready to carry its passengers to some distant location. Her shock and curiosity deepened . . . *A train to where?*

CHAPTER THREE

The truck turned sharply, forcing Ariel to grab the sides of her crate to stabilize herself. Seconds later, she felt the vehicle dropping downwards and concluded there must be several levels inside the mountain. Moving back toward her viewing ports, she watched industrial buildings passing by, thinking this must be the supply area for the city. The vehicle slowed and pulled into a broad open area that contained hundreds of crates stacked together.

Ariel steadied herself inside her wooden container, preparing for the unloading process. Her crate was shoved to the truck bed edge, captured by the forklift and transported gingerly to a waiting pile of similar crates. She had made sure her crate was positioned carefully before loading, hoping that it would be unloaded and positioned without other crates piled on top of it. The plan almost proved successful. To her dismay, she realized one 200 lb. crate had been placed on top of her's.

Suppressing a rising panic, Ariel considered her situation: She could hear worker's voices speaking Spanish, and her heart skipped a beat as she began to worry that her crate might be moved into a refrigerated room, since she was likely located in a food receiving area. That scenario needed to be avoided at all costs. What next? she asked herself. It was now mid-afternoon; best to wait until quitting time—if there was such a thing where there was no sun to tell day from night. Did they have a regular workday, or was it a 24-hour operation?

As she waited, anxiety took its toll. Her muscles ached from hours of tight compression, her head slipped against the side of the box, and her mind drifted. The steady, melodic cadence of voices lulled her to sleep.

Four hours later, Ariel awoke groggy and shaken—not knowing where she was. Quickly reassembling the events of the day, she remembered that she had to find a way to exit the crate. Glancing through her viewing port, it appeared she was alone. This is it— time to go, she told herself. But the challenge of lifting the heavy container piled above her was daunting. It's a physics problem, she concluded; it's a matter of leverage. She needed to raise both her crate's lid and the crate above her high enough to slip through the opening. As Ariel pondered her dilemma, she took one final look through her viewing ports, aware that she could only view a small portion of the area around her. There might be others present whom she couldn't see. She'd just have to chance it. She removed a small saw from her tool kit and began to cut two short pieces from the wooden slats inside her crate to use as braces.

When ready, Ariel summoned her strength and silently hoped that her yoga flexibility and weight training would protect her from injury. She unlatched the lid fasteners and pressed her shoulders against the crate's top. Slowly, the upper container began to rise and slide backward. It lodged against something behind it and stopped, but Ariel had gained the space she needed. Positioning the braces, she carefully lowered the lid. She held her breath and waited. The supports held. Ariel squeezed her pack through the opening and shimmied out of the container, landing on the cold concrete floor. She was free. She stood up and looked around. It appeared she was alone, at least for the moment. But she had to hide the evidence. After removing the wooden braces and stashing them in the crate, she lowered the lid back into place and smiled approvingly. Everything looked normal, no evidence here that anything had happened.

She looked around, amazed at the immense size of the receiving area. It was easily an acre in size with a roof height of seventy feet. The walls were lined with rows of shelving filled with boxes and mechanical equipment. It reminded her of a giant warehouse. But this one had enough food and other resources to last for decades.

Then she heard the voice: male, authoritative, and distinctly hostile. "You there . . . Freeze!"

CHAPTER FOUR

A wave of disappointment swept through Ariel like a cold wind. Not so soon, she thought. This isn't fair. Obeying the verbal instructions coming from behind, she remained still, focusing on the sharp cadence of approaching footsteps. Two sets, she concluded, from the asymmetry of the sound. The uniformed men approached, weapons drawn. No chance of resisting; just play along.

"Raise your hands and turn around slowly," came the harsh order.

When the men saw they were dealing with a young woman, they relaxed.

"Are you an agricultural worker?" one of the men asked, his voice bristling with practiced authority.

"Yes. Working on food transport."

"I need to see your ID." He removed a hand-held scanning device from a waist holster. "Give me your wrist."

Ariel stretched out her arms, knowing she had no such ID.

The man seemed confused. He grabbed her right arm and scanned it with a hand-held device. The scanner beeped several times, indicating negative results.

"No implanted ID chip? What are you doing here?"

"I'm from the outside," said Ariel, now feeling slightly more confident with the situation.

"How did you get in here?"

"I came with one of the trucks . . . to help unload."

The man turned to his companion. "Fallon, call security and tell them we've got an outsider here."

He returned to Ariel and ordered, "Turn around."

Ariel complied and felt the man's hands grab hers and lock a set of plastic handcuffs on her wrists.

"Bring her pack," the man said to his companion as he walked toward the waiting SUV. His partner pushed Ariel forward and shoved her into the back seat of the vehicle. It was equipped with a cage-like barrier that separated her from them. As the vehicle sped through the tunnel, Ariel examined her situation. This was to be expected, she told herself. She just had to be smart and tough.

Fifteen minutes later, the vehicle arrived at a security station. A stern woman in uniform approached, indicating with hand motions for Ariel to exit the vehicle and enter the building. Once inside, Ariel passed rooms filled with workers seated behind desks staring at computers and shuffling papers. The female guard pulled Ariel by her arm down a long hallway that led to a series of identical metal doors. As they reached the last one, the guard punched a code into the electronic lock. The door clicked open. The guard spun Ariel around and removed her handcuffs. "This is your room, girl. It's not the Hilton. There's a bottle of water, a camping pad, and a bowl in there. You'll have plenty of time to think." The guard pushed Ariel into the cell and closed the door. It locked with depressing certainty.

Ariel was now alone in the silence. She looked around. Three walls were made of constructed material, a kind of cement. The fourth wall was raw stone and dirt, the cavern's original underground soil. She felt the dirt. Moisture seeped across her fingers with a distinct coolness. Water oozed from the wall. Glancing upwards, she noticed that much of the ceiling was made of earthen material. Dripping water plopped onto the floor, creating tiny pools and rivulets.

Ariel gathered up the camping pad, propped it against the dirt wall and sat down. Now what? She took a deep breath and shifted into her remote viewing mode, sending her mind outward in concentric circles, attempting an overview scan. Gradually, an image began to assemble itself—an architectural drawing of the interior of the mountain. Different-sized squares and circles, irregular areas and long horizontal spaces filled her mind. The images were hazy at first and then came clear. She gasped at the enormity of it all. It seemed to stretch for miles into the center of the mountain. So extreme. So many questions . . .

And then the room went dark.

CHAPTER FIVE

As Ariel sat dejected in the darkness, a high-level meeting was taking shape several miles away. A dozen sleek, executive jets had materialized in the Canadian skies. In an orderly fashion they set down one-by-one on a private runway on the valley floor. The pilots were directed to arrange their exotic aircraft in a precise line beside their host's $65 million Gulfstream G650. Limousines waited in front of the terminal building to ferry the privileged passengers to their destination—Garrett Henry's luxury residence carved into a nearby mountainside overlooking Lake Albion.

The limos commenced their climb up the long, mountain driveway and approached the expansive complex of buildings. The grand stone, glass and log construction never failed to impress. As the guests began arriving at the main lodge, uniformed service workers directed them to spacious individual cottages in which they could rest and prepare for the upcoming meeting.

Two hours later, Garrett Henry greeted each guest personally as they entered the hardwood-paneled conference room and settled into plush swivel chairs that surrounded a long, oval table. A room-length glass wall overlooked the spectacular lake-in-valley scene. Garrett Henry's close-cropped silver hair and designer dress shirt with light-catching diamond cufflinks spoke of his wealth. He wasted no time in getting down to business. Henry stepped to the front of the room and placed his two hands on the table, leaned forward, and scanned his audience with hard-focused intensity. Along a side wall, a digital screen displayed images of several prototype Universal Energy-powered cars and trucks. His eyes burned with an internal fury.

"It happened faster than anyone thought possible," he said, his voice booming louder than necessary for the size of the room. "The public unveiling of the Universal Energy technology at the Detroit Convention Center has rocked world financial institutions to their core. It's 'game over' for the fossil fuel industry. We expect to take a major loss on our investments."

The screen switched to still photographs of pipeline projects, tar sands and fracking operations, deep ocean drilling operations, coal strip mines and liquefied natural gas terminals in various stages of production or construction—all now threatened with premature extinction. The meeting began to take on the atmosphere of a wake.

"To make matters worse," he exclaimed, "the automobile companies have seized on the opportunity to sell millions of Universal Engine-powered replacement vehicles. Factories have already started to shift their assembly lines over to the new power systems. Stocks in mines, wells, refineries, public electric utilities and freight railroads have tanked, now that it's clear there's no need to mine, transport or burn coal, oil or gas. It's a financial bloodbath."

The new economic reality Garrett Henry described meant that trillions of dollars of stranded assets were now left to wither on the vine. For those whose portfolios were fossil fuel heavy, this astonishing realization foretold unspeakable financial consequences. Not surprisingly, the geopolitical world had been torn asunder. Nothing would be the same and no one knew quite what to expect.

But Garrett Henry, always prepared to seize economic advantage, was ready to reveal his Plan B. "Of course we knew we couldn't burn it all. But we wanted to make the transition on *our* schedule, when *we* were ready." Garrett Henry's fist met the conference table with a loud *thunk,* his voice rising to a snarl. Several participants seated around the table reacted with involuntary physical spasms.

"How bad are the losses?" asked the man seated to his right.

"To Globechek's fossil portfolio? I'd estimate about 18 trillion Euros, split about evenly between reserves and infrastructure. But here's the thing . . ." Garrett straightened up and walked toward the glass wall overlooking the lake. Letting the seconds slip by for added drama, he turned and faced the gathering. "Oil, gas and coal is nice stuff to have around to make heat, light, electricity and so on, but you *can* live without fossil fuels if you have to . . . and mankind did so for a very long time."

The group waited expectantly for the other shoe to drop. Garrett paced the length of the room, his hands locked behind his back, gazing into the distance. When he reached the end of the table and all in the room had swiveled their chairs to follow him, he dropped the bombshell. "*We* are going to own and control that which is *not* optional, that which every man, woman and child must have every day regardless of cost and regardless of quality. And *we* will determine who gets it and who doesn't." Garrett walked over to the conference table grabbed a glass of clear liquid that was placed in front of each person. He held it up for all to see. He twirled the sweating glass around in his hand, staring intensely into it. "*Water* . . . Unlike oil, there is no substitute for water. Without water there is no food, without water there is no life. Those who control the planet's freshwater can control the world's population . . . as well as the world's politics and economics. Ladies and gentlemen, our financial future is *water*—and no one can stop us."

CHAPTER SIX

The room erupted in applause and Garrett Henry was satisfied. He loved drama; he loved how his wealth, influence and political power could be wielded to impress even those who have long enjoyed every thing and every experience unlimited money can buy. Like a circus showman, he launched into his pitch, his voice full of portent. "Climate change and global warming provide us with unprecedented opportunities for financial gain. The hell with fossil fuels! They were a dead end anyway. We all knew that. They were just a temporary means to an end."

He strode across the front of the room and turned toward his spellbound audience, his eyes burning with premeditated intent. "Each one of you will focus your operations on buying up water rights, water utilities, natural springs, lakes, wells, and already privatized water systems . . . any and all the sources of water you can find and the delivery infrastructure as well."

His voice rose with fervor. "I expect us to have complete control over the global market for freshwater within five years. We'll establish futures markets and other derivative water-based financial instruments—puts, calls, swaps—both exchange-traded and over the counter . . . Water as an asset class will become the single most important global physical commodity, dwarfing oil, copper, agriculture and precious metals."

A lean man dressed in perfectly pressed pants and shirt, likely purchased from Savile Row in London, spoke up. "What makes you think they're all going to be willing to sell? There will be resistance. Remember the Cochabamba protests."

"The answer, Marlowe, is because they will have no choice. We are going to squeeze the financial system by further manipulating capital markets. Cash-strapped municipal governments and other water system operators will become unable to operate their systems or build new ones. As unemployment skyrockets and governments begin to fail, they'll seek additional funds to avoid bankruptcy and local uprisings. We'll be more than happy to manage and operate their systems and guarantee the necessary water delivery—on our terms, of course. And, as a matter of fact, I'm already well into the process with bids on a dozen highly stressed cities and countries."

Garrett Henry stepped up to a chart of global farmland fixed to the wall. "The other non-optional element here is food—you can't grow food without water." He pointed at selected parts of the map. "Here in red superimposed on the green areas are the farmlands we're already purchased—in Ukraine, Russia, Africa, and South America. And, of course, we'll control the water sources for those lands. People will have to spend more for food and water since we'll control all the pricing."

"And if they can't afford it?" asked a silver-haired woman.

"Well, that's their problem, isn't it? And that plays to our not-so-secret agenda—to reduce the world population to a reasonable level—under a billion, about where it was in 1800."

Garrett Henry glanced wistfully through the big windows at the valley below. "Imagine . . . less than a billion not so long ago, eight billion now. Clearly, we have way too many people chasing after too few resources. You can see this in the global refugee problem. And the earth is heating up, which is only making things worse."

He pivoted suddenly, "But this is where the opportunity is the greatest: the warmer the world, the greater the environmental and resource problems will become—and our profit potential will explode off the charts. We'll make fortunes in selling off what's left in minerals as the prices rise exponentially; our investments in insurance companies will increase in value as more climate disasters occur and policies become more expensive; our construction companies will reap huge profits in building sea walls and relocating cities to cope with sea-level rise; our seed companies will cash in on the need for new drought-resistant crops. Zoos will become even more popular, as they'll be the only place where people can go to see lions, tigers and bears, and epidemics will generate fortunes for our pharmaceutical and health care companies."

His pacing stopped. His mouth registered a subtle grin. He knew he had his audience in the palm of his hand. Employing his best dramatic posturing, he readied himself to reveal the glorious thought that had just jumped into his head. "You know . . . I could write a book about this—I'd call it 'How to Capitalize on Catastrophe.'"

"Or maybe," the woman suggested, "'How to profit from the end of the world.'"

Garrett Henry was quick on the rebound. "For the 80 or 90 percent of the population, yes, it *is* the end of things. For us it's just the beginning . . ."

He scanned his speechless crowd and generated a twisted smile that would intimidate a bull rattlesnake. "It really doesn't get much better than this."

CHAPTER SEVEN

The cell was so devoid of light that Ariel was unable to see her hands in front of her face, and without the flashlight, food, and other equipment in her pack, she felt helpless. A sharp chill climbed across her shoulders—fear. Instinctively, she stretched out her arms and shook them. As the drips of moisture from the ceiling struck her skin, she felt the cool comfort. Mercifully, it distracted her.

Ariel opened her eyes wide and noticed a dim glow where the water had gathered on her wrists and arms. She reached against the bottom of the wall where water had collected and pressed her hand into the slippery liquid. She removed her jacket and rubbed the water on her bare arms and shoulders, and slowly, her body began to produce just enough light to reveal the outlines of the room. Ariel smiled, remembering that, under the right conditions, water could activate the energy in her skin chloroplasts that had stored sunlight inside their cell membranes. It was a strange and curious feature the human photosynthesizers noticed whenever they found themselves in an exceptionally dark space. They often joked among themselves, calling each other "human fireflies." Now that ability was coming in handy.

But something else was happening. It was more than the usual glow of bioluminescence, common with certain oceanic forms of algae. As Ariel's eyes adjusted, she noticed a sparkle that resulted when she ran her hand across the water on her arm. She sensed that something wanted her attention. Closing her eyes and slipping into her psychic mind for an explanation, a burst of visual information streamed toward her. Images of primordial gases coalesced into star clusters and formed embryonic galaxies, and errant bundles of icy star-matter spun into the far reaches of space. A grey planet materialized, enriched with hydrogen and oxygen and a multitude of life-giving components. In a time-lapse sequence it began to turn blue. This transparent liquid was held together by invisible forces and imbued with unknown power and mysterious physics. Water had appeared on Planet Earth as a stupendous gift from the universe.

Then the story of life commenced: Forces of light, heat and minerals danced together and molecules merged. And after a billion years of experimentation in the primordial ooze, simple microbes appeared. These new evolutionary pioneers then set about laying a foundation for the Tree of Life. Ariel watched with rapt fascination as the great drama played out on her mental screen like a documentary film: primitive bacteria, algae, fungi, horseshoe crabs, turtles, dinosaurs, sunflowers, orchids, hummingbirds, zebras, snowy owls, spinach, tigers, horses, redwood trees . . . and lastly, much, much later—humans.

As the cornucopia of life reeled past her, certain organisms would flash red and slowly dissolve. Sometimes, entire blocks of life-forms would vanish in a heartbeat. This happened five times. As the images of modern-day plants and animals appeared to her, the rate of dissolution began to increase dramatically. Ariel opened her eyes and slowly rubbed her arms. The sparkles were gone. She swallowed hard as she contemplated the message she was receiving—an indication of a much-faster-than-normal rate of extinction. She found herself experiencing unfathomable sadness—grieving the loss of countless species, which she'd never come to know.

But it was not just the loss of the creatures themselves that threatened to sink her into a black oblivion; it was the erasing of the possibility for future relationship between human and other-than-human species. Ariel then remembered how the creation stories of indigenous cultures told of animals teaching humans the methods and morals of balanced and successful living, and how plants generously make food and medicine available to all.

As Ariel traveled through this extraordinary story of Life On Earth she wondered: Who or what is speaking to me? The answer came quickly to her hyper-receptive mind—*water*. Of course, water made it possible for all life-forms to come into existence; water sustained them for eons. But now so many are gone. Extinct.

And then she wondered: What if water remembers? Since I'm 70 percent water, is water sharing its memories with me?

CHAPTER EIGHT

Bands of sunlight flooded the glass windows in Garrett Henry's office. He silently reflected on the agricultural, food processing and servicing operations he had created, not just in the Albion valley, but inside the nearby cavernous mountain as well. He reveled in knowing that a comfortable future for hundreds of select men and women would be assured in his underground refuge enclave, no matter what happened in the outside world. He was sure billions would perish from the implosions of global economies, roiling waves of homeless and landless people and collapsing nation-states. But it wouldn't happen overnight, he mused. Rebellions and revolutions would occur, indeed, they had already started. And people would fight to the end—they always did. Weapons of mass destruction would likely be used and millions incarcerated. The die was cast. It would be survival of the fittest, and in reality that meant those with the most money, influence, and power.

Garrett Henry's wealth was not the kind of wealth one person could ever legitimately earn in a lifetime. Henry had been handed a life of ease and limitless resources thanks to his family's multi-generational connections with the shadowy subsets of governments. His forefathers had crafted the protocols that fleeced many a hapless colony of natural resources and human capital. As WWII was winding down, Garrett Henry's father shrewdly managed to persuade British Intelligence to appoint him as the director of a classified project whose mission was to locate and retrieve hidden Nazi and Japanese loot.

The men of Operation Roundabout and Silver Scepter did, in fact, recover vast caches of gold bullion, precious gems and priceless art stolen from museums and personal collections throughout Europe and Asia. The Axis Powers had collected these high-value artifacts during their failed quest for global domination. However, a sizable portion of the stupendous hauls mysteriously disappeared into various governmental and favored private-sector hands.

Immediately following the recovery of the wartime booty in the late 1940's, Garrett Henry Sr. and his financial partners shunted a portion of the funds into a multitude of black budgets and hidden accounts distributed around the world. The funds were then invested in the development of advanced technology, some of it inspired by, or acquired from, sources that officially do not exist.

Spectacular profits generated from the manufacturing and sale of these advanced technologies found their way into international investments in fossil fuels, real estate, banking sleights-of-hand, counterfeit bond sales and other nefarious ventures. Some researchers claimed that the members of the clandestine financial cabal controlled assets worth at least $40 to $50 trillion.

Garrett Henry Jr., as one of the fortunate beneficiaries of these epic monetary manipulations, was personally determined to carry on the tradition of growing the fund by adding several new decimal points to its future balance. Consequently, Henry and his select network of associates were quietly amassing most of the world's physical and financial wealth, and building their own survival villages and equipping them sufficiently to weather the coming storms caused by the actions of desperate humans, nature's fury or . . . something else equally calamitous.

As mastermind and director of the cabal's global operations, Garrett Henry was preparing for a teleconference with his marketing team to announce a new agricultural product. Henry activated the electric shutters on his broad windows to darken the spacious room and allow for high-contrast viewing on the wall-mounted screen. He paced back and forth across the hardwood floor in front of the screen as befitted his obsessive nature. Six separate live video views of the half-dozen participants located around the world appeared on the display.

As was typical, Henry was calling the shots. "Our agricultural products division—ChemAgCo—has just completed field trials of a new pesticide. They're calling it 'FarmX'. It's made from some of the same chemicals in what was known as Agent Orange. I want all of you to instruct your regional dealers to replace the old inventory with the new product. It's more powerful and effectively destroys just about every damn living thing that comes near the crop."

The dealer from India spoke up. "What about collateral damage? Environmental impacts? Human health issues? There's going to be pushback from the regulators and environmental organizations."

Henry responded, "What choice do farmers have? The pests have mutated so much we have to nuke them; otherwise farmers would have no crop at all. It's an end game now, my friends, and that's not a bad thing, as we know. If crops fail, people die. So we say to them: Buy our product—if you can afford it, and you might get a few more years of decent yields. Of course, we know that over time, the environment will become too polluted to support life, but it's the same result—systemic collapse and we're closer to our goal of a reduced-population planet. We just need to make sure we don't eat any of that food."

Garrett turned toward the screen. "By the way, our organic gardens in the valley are doing very well. Bumper crop this year. We're storing it inside the mountain, freeze drying it, canning, building up the stocks. I think you've all seen the aquaponics video; the new expanded facility is really cranking—plenty of high quality fish, unlimited supply."

The Asian representative again spoke up. "Agriculture needs water. Wells are going dry all over India and China, and groundwater is becoming depleted. In some places, water from the glaciers is almost gone."

"It's the same in Syria, Iran and elsewhere in the Middle East," remarked the rep from Turkey. "Ground and surface water is running out."

Henry's voice took on a sharper edge. "We own access to most of those remaining major freshwater sources now, don't we? I've released billions to all of you to purchase those rights."

"Well," the rep from Turkey hedged, "It hasn't exactly worked out that way. The governments were willing and we guaranteed them generous amounts of personal cash, but the size of the public demonstrations shocked us. People see water as a public right and are willing to put their lives on the line for it. Dozens have died already from battles with local police and army units. It's a dicey situation."

Garrett pondered the statement. "They'll cave—the demonstrators, when they see they have no choice if they want water, and they'll find out quickly that they're outgunned and outmaneuvered by our security forces. We have all the resources, they don't. We can wait, they can't."

A pause prevailed as the conference participants absorbed Henry's sober comment. The regional dealer from Africa spoke up. "We've encountered something a little different in Africa. It seems an organization called the American Climate Justice Collaborative is giving local communities and villages money to purchase their own water rights, and they're providing technicians to help them install new wells and water purification and sanitation systems. They're also working in urban areas. Wherever they show up, they try to bid against us, but they rarely succeed. They must have access to substantial funding. What do you know about them?"

Garrett's eyes pinched down. "It's that liberal do-gooder guy in the Midwest—Walter Langenstein. And damn if he isn't using my own money against me. If he wants war, that's what he'll get." As he contemplated his counter-strategy, Garrett stared at the errant light beams from outside that attempted to infiltrate his conference room. He leaned against a desk and addressed his teleconference audience. "His financial resources are limited. I know he's got $20 billion to work with, but we can outspend him 1,000 to 1. We'll crush him—he can't last. And just to make life more difficult for him, I'll have our special-ops team pay him a not-so-friendly visit."

Garrett's speech was interrupted by an insistent tone emanating from the mobile phone on his desk. "Excuse me, it's security. I told them to check in with me regularly."

Garrett Henry retrieved the phone and read the text message: *Security breach. Have retained a young woman without Mountain ID. Placed in solitary confinement. Awaiting further instructions.*

CHAPTER NINE

The City of Milwaukee

The circular lobby of the American Climate Justice Collaborative headquarters featured a tile-inlaid floor that displayed the planet's colorful biodiversity of life. This stunning mosaic recalled the great drama of evolution, beginning 4.6 billion years ago when temperatures were boiling hot and the atmosphere was chock full of carbon dioxide. Over a distance of twenty feet, visitors would progress through the subsequent eons, eras and epochs, finally arriving in the present age— the unofficial Anthropocene—which depicted both verdant forests and poisoned industrial wastelands: regrettably, the 'signs of the times.'

The sleek steel, stone, and glass LEED Platinum building had breathed new life into the neighborhood of century-old masonry architecture. It invited a brighter future for the surrounding aging structures—tough, rugged, utilitarian, long-vacant ghost factories, patiently awaiting new tenants in the industrial district of downtown Milwaukee.

An international delegation had come to meet with Walter Langenstein, wealthy manufacturing magnate and social justice philanthropist, whose dream project had finally taken physical form. The ACJC was the nerve center for the planning and disbursing of $20 billion, with projects focused on urgent climate change issues and quality-of-life factors for marginalized populations around the globe.

The mission of the ACJC, according to Walter Langenstein, was to focus the world's attention on the actions needed to avert some of the worst-case impacts of a conflict-ridden, global-warmed planet. The ACJC's prescriptions were ambitious:

Number One: Elimination of the use of fossil fuels for energy production. Number Two: Dramatic reduction of consumption of factory-farmed meat and dairy products. Number Three: Elimination of deforestation and the development of aggressive programs for reforestation. Number Four: Strong encouragement of a one-biological-child-per-couple policy. (For high-carbon footprint couples, a near-zero reproduction rate is recommended.) Number Five: Implementation of substantial wealth taxes, including a tax on international money transfers. Number Six: Rapid reduction of resource consumption in affluent countries. Number Seven: Advocacy of a 30 to 50% cut in global military expenditures.

The ACJC received plenty of pushback on its recommendations. Walter commonly responded by stressing that unless humans commit to a more sustainable relationship with the planet, nature would do the culling. "Remember," he would remind the skeptics, "If we fail to take action on our own, the earth will attempt to return to homeostasis or natural balance—but it will be a very hot, hostile, lonely and barren future planet—not fit for human habitation."

Enthusiastic student interns greeted the delegation. As soon as everyone was seated in the auditorium, Walter Langenstein stepped to the center of the stage. His statesman-like-presence gave powerful gravitas to his precise and forcefully spoken words, "Friends, I can now announce that 80 to 90 percent of our remaining fossil fuels will remain in the ground. Universal Energy now renders fossil fuels unnecessary for energy production." A loud cheer punctuated by vigorous applause followed Walter's good news.

Ever since the surprise introduction of a dozen Universal Energy-powered cars, trucks and SUVs at the Detroit Convention Center, the geopolitics of the world were in turmoil. Amazingly, the media had even ignored the usual mindless antics of rich and famous celebrities to endlessly speculate about how the world would cope with this marvelous, new technology. Major carmakers were flooding the media with ads for a new generation of cars and trucks, and it was boom times for manufacturers and installers of Universal Energy generators.

But the future appeared less rosy for others. For those who built fortunes on the black gold, it was clear the grand gusher of global oil revenues would soon dwindle to a trickle. Royal families in Middle Eastern countries feared they could no longer contain the mullahs who depended on generous subsidies. Countries formerly fat with hydrocarbon reserves and fossil profits were finding themselves devoid of leverage and now functionally irrelevant. Terrorist organizations funded with oil- and gas-based largesse were frantically looking elsewhere for support. Now that the oil lanes in the Middle East and the gas lines in Eastern Europe no longer needed protection, the U.S. military was about to lose its day job. Given that oil was no longer the kingpin of concern driving world politics and seemingly endless wars, attention was rapidly shifting to something more fundamental. And that something had the potential to become even more contentious.

A thunderous applause greeted Mrs. Maribel Maluum, the representative from the Democratic Republic of Congo, as she stepped up to the podium and adjusted the microphone to match her height. Above and to the right of her, a video depicted a forlorn setting in Africa—a wind-swept brown field of dirt inhabited by several severely dehydrated cows. The camera panned across the dry landscape that swirled with dust as a Land Rover bounced along a rutted, dirt road. The camera zoomed in on the vehicle, which slowed to avoid a ragged line of young African women walking in the opposite direction. Most of the women were carrying scuffed, yellow plastic three- and five-gallon jerry cans on their heads or using straps that distributed the weight of the jugs on their backs to their foreheads. They stared at the riders in the in the truck, eyes wide, empty, and exhausted.

"This is what women do every day," said Mrs. Maluum, her voice filling the room. "Sometimes twice a day. Have you tried to lift a twenty-liter (five-gallon) jug of water? It weighs about eighteen kilograms or forty pounds. Twenty liters doesn't go very far in a family. Worldwide, women and children spend 200 million hours daily collecting water."

In the next scene, the truck pulled up next to an oasis with a small pond. A dozen women and girls wearing brightly-colored dresses had gathered together and were talking rapidly. Half the group was standing in the shallow end of the pond dunking their jugs in the brown, opaque water. At the upper end of the pond stood five emaciated cows.

"This is the nearest water source," continued Mrs. Maluum. "You can see it's not clean. Every day they must make the three or four hour trek, which means the girls don't have time for school. We know a young girl's education is the best way to slow population growth. If they can't stay in school, they don't learn what's possible for them in life and how to space their pregnancies . . . or the benefits of refraining from child-bearing completely. And hauling the water is dangerous, often exposing them to rape and kidnapping."

Mrs. Maluum's audience observed the scene in stunned silence, clearly troubled. A man in the audience asked, "Why don't they drill wells?"

"Wells are extremely expensive. Even basic maintenance costs too much for a village to afford. People here live on about a $1.25 U.S. a day. In fact, if an American were to pay a proportional amount of money for a bottle of clean water, it would cost about $30. Digging a well would cost about $300,000. A $1,000 repair cost for a well would be the equivalent of $100,000 in the U.S. So you see it's completely unaffordable in terms of the local economy. That's why we're here—to find ways to help people in our country develop clean water sources."

"That water looks pretty bad to me," noted a woman in the crowd. "I'm assuming it makes people sick."

"Of course. You saw the cows in the pond. The surface water is contaminated with bacteria from humans and animals, and wells often contain high levels of arsenic and fluoride. I run a health clinic that treats people every day for water-borne diseases. Globally, almost one million people die each year from a water-related illness and 750-million lack access to clean water. Bad water takes a very heavy toll on children—about one every twenty seconds. Chronic sickness robs people of their ability to learn and generate income, and what little money they have is spent treating the illness."

The video faded to black. The tragic nature of the subject matter left no room for applause.

"So you need more wells and water purification equipment," said Walter.

"That's a big part of it. And we need money to build sanitation systems and train local people. They need to be able to do their own water quality testing and maintain their water systems."

"How about electricity?"

"We need generators to run the clinics and the schools, to provide energy for cooking and to enable Internet connections—all things you take for granted in America."

"You've established health clinics," added Walter. "You're making a difference."

"It's a start," said Mrs. Maluum. "But it may not last. There's conflict just over the border, and it looks like it's coming our way. Climate change has drastically altered the rainfall patterns, so people aren't able to grow enough food, so it's starve or steal someone else's food. That's what's happening. I expect we may be forced to abandon our homes and fields, like so many before us." Mrs. Maluum looked away into the distance, deeply troubled.

"I think we can help," Walter offered.

Walter announced to the delegations that their meeting would resume in an hour. He then led the DRC team through the offices and conference areas of the ACJC. Walter directed Mrs. Maluum's attention to the many staff members representing different nationalities. "We're all here for the same reason," he said, "to develop and implement creative ways to meet the pressing and extraordinary challenges that lie ahead. We must succeed. If not, we'll join the long list of failed species—it's as simple as that."

They continued on into the 5,000 sq. ft. space that housed the design and testing lab for water purification equipment. Walter introduced Harrison Featherway who demonstrated how Universal Energy generators could power water treatment equipment by using the water itself as fuel.

The African delegation had many questions about the variety of purification systems—which ones would best address certain problems and how they might be purchased. ACJC staff members explained how the technology eliminated harmful bacteria and viruses, and removed parasites, pesticides, pharmaceuticals and heavy metals from water sources without requiring chemicals or carbon-based fuels.

As Walter finished extolling the virtues of the technology, Mrs. Maluum turned to Walter. She was blunt: "I think it's fine how you're trying to help people in developing countries, but you Americans are the greedy ones who are messing everything up."

"I know," uttered Walter, anticipating what she was about to say.

"I see it like this." Mrs. Maluum set her feet firmly on the floor and started gesturing with her hands. The sides of her long, multicolored sleeves swayed back and forth with her arms. "Imagine we were invited to lunch at a fancy restaurant. The Americans arrive in a couple of big limousines. My people arrive by foot, or maybe we rode the bus for forty-five minutes to get there. Then we all sit down at the table together. The Americans order expensive wine to get started, then a nice green salad and maybe some fat shrimp for appetizers. The Americans are served lobster or prime rib for the main course along with some organic vegetables. We get served glasses of water and a small bowl of rice, but the water looks suspect cause it's slightly yellow and there's some brown specs floating around in it . . . Maybe there's a few pieces of goat meat in the rice. We all eat our lunch. Then the waiter brings desserts for the Americans that look like something out of a fairy tale. The Americans each pick one or two. The waiter doesn't even look at us. When the Americans are finished, we're asked to split the check. They turn to us and say 'have a good day' and leave. That's how it is."

Walter was listening intently and offered no immediate response.

"So you lecture us about reducing our populations, but you Americans use at least fifty to seventy times more resources per person than someone in my country. You need to stop using so much stuff, otherwise there won't be anything left for the rest of us—and we've been waiting a long time. We have to learn to share with each other, otherwise we'll all perish."

"I completely agree," Walter said, engaging Mrs. Maluum directly. "But it's not an easy sell. Those who have the stuff don't want to give it up . . . and those who don't have it yet, want it." As he spoke, Walter felt his own guilt rising to the surface.

Mrs. Maluum raised her voice, "I know you've raised $20 billion. That's a good start. And it's great that this new energy technology can be used anywhere, but our countries are collapsing and our people are dying from disease. There are millions of refugees living in crowded camps and trying to escape into other countries, and wars are being fought over land and minerals. But as we speak, foreign business people in our countries are purchasing rights to our agricultural land, removing that land from traditional use and privatizing our water systems. Many *hundreds* of billions are needed to address the problems—probably trillions."

"Well, I—" Walter started to respond but his mobile phone began ringing. He removed it from his pocket and glanced at the caller ID. "Excuse me," he said to the DRC delegation. "I have to take this call."

Walter gestured to his assistant director and asked her to continue meeting with the DRC delegates. "Make sure all their questions are answered and they receive whatever support they need."

Walter sought privacy, as he knew the call had originated from the head of his security team. Glancing back at the delegates who were now observing Harrison Featherway demonstrate a Universal Energy-powered water purification device, Walter had a hard time believing what he was hearing. On the other end of the line, his chief security officer informed Walter that his estate had just been attacked, several staff had been killed and a fire was raging out of control.

"How—?" Walter struggled to ask.

"Some kind of special-ops group," replied the officer. "It seems they knew their way around. We notified the police, but they said it's too dangerous for you to return."

CHAPTER TEN

"Walter, what is it?" From across the room, Catherine Connelly observed the alarm register on Walter's face. She was reminded of his distress when the New Century Engine Plant was bombed seven months ago.

"Another bombing. This time it's my estate. We need a strategy, Cath. It's seems war has been declared, and I think I know who's behind it."

Walter offered his sincere apologies to the DRC delegates, saying he needed to attend to an urgent matter. He called together his allies: Catherine, Jake, Snapdragon, Razr and Harrison. Like a football quarterback huddling his team on the field prior to a critical play, he issued his instructions: "Catherine will ride with Snapdragon; the rest of you will travel with me. My estate has been attacked. Proceed immediately to the *Opportunity*. We'll talk there. Code Red. And Snapdragon, check for tails."

Snapdragon's midnight-black Dodge Charger growled with a fierce, electrical whine as it leapt up the concrete exit ramp from the underground garage like a prizefighter entering the ring. With a rush of Universal Energy torque, it pounced onto the busy street skidding sideways to avoid an oncoming municipal bus. Catherine's head flew back against the headrest, but Snapdragon was in her element and happy to have the power of 298 kilowatts

(400 horsepower) of instant torque at her command. The Charger, though, had to cool its heels as it entered the slower lanes of city traffic. Catherine scanned the array of screens on the dashboard. "It's like a TV studio in here," she noted. "How can you drive and watch all these screens?"

"They serve different purposes," Snapdragon said, her voice dropping suddenly as she glanced into her rear view mirror. She then reached over and touched a periscope graphic on the video display. The screen displayed a camera-like device rising from the top of the vehicle's roof and pointing itself behind them. Snapdragon touched the portion of the image that showed a white van with several antennas about five car-lengths behind them. Cross hairs appeared over the van. The screen then displayed an enlarged image of the mysterious van.

"We're being followed."

"That white van?" asked Catherine.

"Yes, but not for long."

The Charger pulled sharply out of the line of traffic and made a left turn that shoved Catherine hard against the passenger-side door. With a burst of acceleration, the car fled down the side street, making turns just as the lights were turning red. The white van, not nearly so nimble, struggled to keep up. Catherine was getting dizzy from Snapdragon's evasive driving tactics.

"I think we lost them," Catherine said hopefully.

"Not really, I'm just trying to buy us some time for counter-measures." Snapdragon pulled the car into a parking lot that offered several exits. She began typing on a small keyboard that emerged from the dashboard. "There—I've created a dummy data bundle that will give them false GPS readings for us, just in case they've attached a GPS tracker to my car. It will send a bogus signal that they'll interpret as us—and get them off our ass. It'll send them to the other side of town. It's a classic feign. That should keep them out of our hair for now. If need be, I can engage the stealth system, something Ewar worked up, that would make us nearly invisible. But that's a dangerous thing to do in traffic because you want other cars to see where you are. It's a last resort measure."

"You're incredible," said Catherine, shaking her head in amazement.

The two women made their way to the Lakefront Yacht Club, south of the city along the western shore of Lake Michigan. The Charger entered the parking lot and wound its way through the Porsches, BMWs, and Tesla Xs. Choosing a space that offered a quick escape across a grassy area, Snapdragon opened the trunk and removed several items, some of which she handed to Catherine—a compact stun gun and pepper spray can. "Here, you might need these. Put them in your backpack," she said matter-of-factly as she removed both a stun gun and a Glock G19 and strapped them into small holsters on her belt. "Just in case someone might have anticipated our presence in the area." She then lifted her long, loose blouse over the firearms, effectively concealing them.

Catherine looked directly at her friend. "I guess we're in fighting mode now . . . again."

"I am. And you?"

"Just as soon as I catch my breath."

The women scanned the harbor. Three 120-foot, slightly raked masts towered over the docks. A cool breeze played across the water. Sounds of gulls flying overhead provided a comforting lakeside ambience. On the surface everything looked and felt normal, but both women remained hyper-alert.

Snapdragon and Catherine paused at the electronic gate. Snapdragon entered the required activation code. The gate clicked open. A white sign with carefully lettered numbers directed them toward Slip Area G. Catherine always felt excitement when approaching the tall ship, but this time apprehension flooded her, given the disturbing news they had just received. Catherine still harbored remnants of trauma, as unknown adversaries had torched her own home in a punitive attack.

Before them loomed the *Opportunity*—190 feet long and built of high-strength carbon-fiber surfaced with 170 feet of hardwood decking. The ship was a sight to behold—with three soaring masts that could hold 9,800 square feet of sail.

To the observer, the *Opportunity* appeared as a 21st century, state-of-the-art vessel that drew upon the elegant and timeless designs of 18th century clipper ships. Though the topside recalled traditional tall ship lines, all its operations were computer-controlled. Its sails could be furled and unfurled in three minutes, while its masts could be retracted downwards almost flush with the deck for purposes of rapid travel if needed. This unusual feature was important, as the ship also featured two hull-length rails stowed below the waterline. The rails could extend from each side of the ship providing lift. With sufficient thrust, the ship would rise upon its rails and achieve speeds of 50 knots (57 mph).

The *Opportunity's* interior reflected the finest in contemporary yacht design, offering teleconferencing spaces equipped with the latest in satellite and wireless communication systems. Moreover, the ship provided comfortable living quarters for up to thirty people, and its stores could supply enough food and supplies for round-the-world voyages. In its hold it carried a minisub. Harrison had converted the twin main engines to plasma electrical generators that could send a total of 18,000 horsepower equivalent to a pair of powerful water jets.

Snapdragon, ever wary, tore her gaze away from the craft, "Come on," she said to Catherine. "Let's not get distracted."

As they approached the boat, they sighted the crew: a dozen men and women dressed in white pants and green fleece-lined canvas jackets standing watch at strategic locations along the ship's broad deck and in its rigging. On the jackets appeared the ship's name—*Opportunity*—flanked by a colorful graphic of a Monarch butterfly.

"Dr. Connelly?" one of the crew called out.

"Yes," answered Catherine.

"We've been expecting you. Follow us please."

They boarded quickly. Snapdragon looked back toward the parking lot to confirm they had not been followed. Noticing a small vibration beneath her feet and six crewmembers casting off lines that held the ship to the dock, she began to dismiss her concerns. Looking upwards, she observed lookouts in the top rigging scanning in all directions with binoculars.

A crewmember led them into a wood-paneled chart room. Catherine had sailed on the *Opportunity* before, but she always marveled at the stunning woodwork. She ran her hands along the wide railing that curved and twisted artistically in the fashion of classic European boatbuilding. The chart room windows were fitted with polished brass hardware embellished with intricate stained glass floral images, and the ceiling radiated elegance with its dark-cherry wooden ribbing. Inside the room, guests could relax in comfortable armchairs while admiring the antique tables. The detailed carpentry was testimony to a rare level of master craftsmanship.

Walter, Jake, Razr and Harrison welcomed them aboard. "I trust you arrived without incident?" Walter said to Catherine.

"Not entirely, we were followed, but Snapdragon took care of that . . . as she usually does."

"We took one of the limos. Nothing unusual," said Walter.

Once settled into their seats and served tea, the team prepared to discuss the attack on Walter's estate.

Walter spoke unevenly, his voice devoid of the passionate, charismatic force that it usually held. He forced his words; they carried his pain. "Under cover of darkness, early this morning, several intruders cut the power to the security system, immobilized my security guards and entered the estate's main complex. They broke into the basement lab and placed several firebombs in the area that were later detonated remotely. I expect they rifled through the contents of our files and likely removed the laptop computers. They also thoroughly searched the room of the staff member I caught spying, probably looking for any data he might have left there . . . It seems they knew their way around."

"Injuries? Casualties?" Jake asked.

"Two guards killed and one in critical condition, several others suffered burns attempting to extinguish the fires, but they put up a good fight."

Walter addressed Snapdragon. "Are we in trouble? Do we have enough backup here?"

Snapdragon had curled her legs into the wide chair. "I try to anticipate things like this. I have a full file of material—all the data Ewar gave us on the Universal Energy generators—here in the project operations room. I always have backup because you never know when your adversaries might strike, and I had a hunch they would—didn't know when or where, though. Good that you have the *Opportunity* as a secondary base."

"Who or what are we dealing with? I'm sure it's Garrett Henry and his Globechek agents. I'm hearing disturbing news from our people in in Europe, Africa, South America and Asia. As you know, the ACJC distributes cash to village and city leaders to help them purchase or buy back local land and water rights. But apparently, secretive companies with very deep pockets are threatening our people. They seem intent on securing control of land and water resources everywhere. In many places, our people and our cash are the only forces standing between local ownership and control and the privatization or exploitation of these essential resources by the Globecheck agents."

"Do we really have enough money to take them on?" asked Catherine.

"No, not by any means. Mrs. Maluum was right when she said that hundreds of billions would be necessary to successfully address the problems of developing countries. We need *a lot* more money."

"But you're giving these guys major heartburn," said Jake attempting to place a positive spin on the discussion.

"Apparently," responded Walter.

"And they're hitting back," added Snapdragon.

"And I worry about Ariel and Debbie and the others," said Catherine. "We still haven't heard from them."

"I'm concerned too," said Razr. "I think they've been taken to someplace that's part of Garrett Henry's operations. Ariel talked about places called 'refuge enclaves.' Her situation could be used against us—like for ransom money, possibly."

"That raises the stakes," said Jake.

"And it also provides opportunity," Snapdragon offered cryptically.

All attention focused on Snapdragon. "We recovered computer records from the room of the staff member we know was a Globechek spy. We've determined he had access to Globechek financial records. I've examined the files and they appear to reference very large sums of money. I believe the data indicates the presence of multiple black budgets and hidden bank accounts that Garrett Henry and his cadre of financial operators have amassed over the years."

Walter's curiosity was now on high alert. "Go on—what are you suggesting?"

"If we could somehow obtain those account numbers, I think I could tap into the accounts and—"

Walter's mind was spinning like a one-arm-bandit slot machine that suddenly parked on five 7s. He interrupted Snapdragon, "And we could redirect that money to humanitarian programs and climate change initiatives. Brilliant Snapdragon! Brilliant."

Snapdragon raised her arms, spreading the palms of her hands. "Whoa, wait a minute. Not easily done. We'd need an insider: someone who can gain access to Globechek's heavily protected computer files . . . and that's certainly not one of us."

A knock on the door of the room caused all heads to turn. "Come in," said Walter.

A female crewmember stepped into the room. "Sorry to interrupt you, Sir. We just received a letter for Dr. Connelly, care of you. Special drone-delivery from the Harbor Postal Service."

Catherine stepped forward to receive the letter. Self-consciously, she proceeded to open the envelope. She removed a folded 4x6-inch greeting card with a watercolor scene of a lake in a valley. Inside, it contained a short note. Catherine read it several times to herself. It said: *AOK. On a mission of discovery.* On the bottom right side of the page were the letters in small script: *DC.*

Jake was becoming impatient. "So what does it say?"

Catherine kept staring at the note. "I think it's in code, but it seems to say Ariel and Debbie are safe and that they're involved in some kind of 'mission of discovery,' whatever that means. It appears that Debbie Chen sent it."

Razr was the first to respond. He spun around in his chair; a broad grin spanned his face. "I think Ariel is spying on that Garrett Henry guy. In fact, I'm sure of it. Snap . . . That's how you're going to get your numbers for the secret bank accounts."

CHAPTER ELEVEN

The cell door opened with a rusty screech. Ariel raised her head and squinted, attempting to cope with the bright light that was pointed at her face. She pushed her tangled hair away to gain a better view of the situation.

"Get up," a woman's stern voice commanded. "You have a visitor."

Ariel staggered to her feet. She had lost five pounds and had been without a shower or a real meal for days. She didn't know how many, as there was no way of keeping track of time. Although she had no access to sunlight, Ariel had been able to extract basic nutrients by moistening her skin with the water that seeped into her cell—that was another physical advantage of being a human photosynthesizer. Still, she was in a seriously weakened condition.

Entering into the lighted hallway produced a surge of energy in Ariel's cells, and her mind quickened. Sensing that a critical event was about to occur, she deployed her psychic skills to help her prepare for what was to come next.

The matron led Ariel into a sparsely furnished room, outfitted with several simple chairs and a small table. The matron left and closed the door behind her.

After a long wait and without warning, a man stepped into the room. Impeccably dressed, he projected a powerful presence. Ariel recognized him. She shifted her mind into overdrive, knowing her words would determine her fate and possibly the fate of others.

"Please be seated, young lady," said the man, gesturing with his arm toward the chairs.

Ariel complied and the man seated himself opposite her.

His eyes locked onto hers. Maximum power to the psychic shields, she commanded her herself.

"This is a restricted facility," the man began. Ariel detected a tone of impatience in his voice. "People who trespass suffer the consequences. I cannot allow you to leave the premises, as operations here must remain secret. But I will make you an offer: I know who you are; you have skills that could be of use to us, and we can place you in a position that I believe you would find fulfilling."

"Can you be more specific?" asked Ariel, sensing it would strengthen her position if she indicated some interest. She found herself surprised that this man deemed her to have some value to his program. On the other hand, she could be stepping into a trap.

"The specifics will be made clear at a later date."

Ariel reviewed her options: They were limited. "What's in it for me if I agree?"

"A longer life . . . outside of solitary confinement." Ariel detected the beginnings of a malicious grin on the man's face, which he quickly extinguished.

Ariel knew she had to play along with his game if she was to achieve freedom. Plus, she really wanted to know more about the nature and purpose of the underground city. It was time to go on the offensive.

"I can't agree to something I know nothing about. I need more information. And by the way, who are you and what or whom do you represent?"

"I am Garrett Henry, Ariel Connelly. If you play nicely, I can guarantee you a fine future. Please bear in mind that there will be many people who soon will *not* know a fine future, and I believe you're aware of that possibility, aren't you?" He glared at her in the silence of the room. Her skin tingled as if she was being compressed and slowly suffocated, like a python crushes its prey. A dizziness threatened to overcome her.

Ariel considered her circumstances: She suspected Henry knew about her skill base and personal background, and most likely he had information about the other members of her team—and certainly Walter Langenstein. She decided she'd need to be careful, very careful.

"I am willing to consider anything that's reasonable."

Garrett Henry laughed. "My dear, you are in no position to dictate what's reasonable to me. You either accept my conditions or spend your lovely youth slowly dissolving away in a dark underground cell. That's the deal."

Tough deal, thought Ariel. Not too much to work with here. She ignored a shudder that fled through her arms and shoulders.

"You make a strong case . . . and my skin cells need sunlight."

Henry stood and approached Ariel, bending down and looked directly into her face. She felt like she was under a microscope. "Oh, so much potential; such a shame to waste your energy on silly things like trying to save the world. The sooner you realize the world as you've known it is doomed, the sooner you can join those who will inherit a new earth—one that is much less crowded and one that is much more enjoyable."

"Is that what you are trying to do?" asked Ariel, trying desperately to marshal her confidence to match his. "Create a kind of breakaway civilization?"

"In effect, yes, but no need to create it. It's already here and functioning quite well, thank you. And I think you've had some experience with it, haven't you?"

Ariel remained silent.

"You could be one of the lucky ones who gets to participate. But the term I would use is something like 'New World Order.' . . . And so, my dear, are you in or not? I need an answer, *now*."

"I'm in. What's next?"

"You'll be shown to your quarters. Instructions will be given later. Good day, young lady. I know you're a smart and reasonable person. You've made a good decision."

Ariel watched Garrett Henry leave the room. Behind him followed an invisible cyclone of energy. She relaxed in her chair, shoulders dropping and breathing heavily, not at all sure what she had agreed to.

CHAPTER TWELVE

Garrett Henry rode the elevator to the top floor of the underground complex. He entered into the front lobby, a broad chamber with walls made of black granite panels. Walking at a fast pace, he approached a woman seated at the reception desk. "I need an encrypted teleconference room."

"Of course, Mr. Henry," the woman said, as she moved a finger across a touch panel screen. "8B is open."

Garrett Henry contacted his thirty-two-year-old nephew, Jason Henry, on the secure private link. "Uncle Garrett, you're calling late. You must be working a big business deal."

"It's still early here . . . Business? No, but a big deal politically. I've taken a hostage."

"Hostage? I don't understand."

"It seems a clever young woman has found her way past our security system and into the mountain. This same woman has close connections with certain people who are causing trouble for us. However, that may soon be a thing of the past now that I have some, shall we say, *additional leverage*."

"What do you plan to do with her?"

"She already knows too much. I've persuaded her to agree to work with us, but that's just a ruse to immobilize her. I need to put her on ice . . . to move her to someplace where she can't be found."

Jason paused before reacting. "So you're probably considering the Oceion Project."

"Indeed I am. I'm so glad we think alike. Oceion 9 needs more workers, so I have an assignment for you. Take charge of her. Pick her up here along with the other workers scheduled to be transported there—and make sure she is sufficiently isolated—until I have need of her. Can I count on you?"

"Of course. I'll leave day after tomorrow, early. I'm still finishing up with Karl. We're signing the acquisition papers for the purchase of the Global-Cola Bottling Company. That will give us access to a lot of good source water . . . I could be in the valley for breakfast on Thursday."

"Good . . . and try to stay under Mach 2 to draw less attention from the Canadian military, will you, especially when you're crossing the border? I don't enjoy making those calls to calm them down."

"I'll take it slow."

It was still dark when Jason Henry's salsa red Jaguar coupe pulled into the New Jersey airport. Operated by the New York Port Authority, the Teterboro Airport was favored by private jet owners, as it was only twelve minutes from downtown Manhattan in good traffic conditions. Jason parked the 500 horsepower Jag in front of the hangar and grabbed his briefcase from the car. Hanger 20 looked like the other hangars, except it was newer, large and completely windowless. A 24/7 security guard ensured that no one except Jason and his close associates could enter the building when the craft was present.

The two guards recognized Jason on sight, but they still demanded a retinal scan. They also asked for his ID and passwords before allowing him access to the hangar. That done, Jason entered the metal building.

The dim overhead lamps weakly outlined the shape of 110-foot wide, two-story triangular airship. Jason approached the edge of the craft, slid his hand across its mirror surface and felt the unusual material radiate rainbows away from his hand and warm to his touch. He patted it affectionately as if it was a personal race-horse he was taking out for a midnight ride. Fifteen minutes later, he was in the pilot's seat and remotely opening the wide hangar doors. With the antigravitics enabled, the craft slid silently forward and cleared the building, floating vertically upwards, slowly at first, to allow Jason to confirm that the sky was clear of incoming or out-going aircraft. Jason took several minutes to clear his takeoff with air-traffic control. The guards watched as the ship, now appearing as a black shadow in the sky, disappeared into the night. Jason set the ARV-2500xi *Skysaber* on a course for the Lake Albion Valley—to meet Ariel Connelly.

❖ ❖ ❖

As Jason had promised his uncle, he did keep the *Skysaber* under Mach 2 (1500 mph), most of the time. Once beyond Lake Superior, while over the wild lands of western Ontario and the southern lakes of Manitoba, he did several brief sprints that took him close to Mach 3. Slowing down as he approached the Canadian Rockies, he covered the 2,860 miles in 1.5 hours. Garrett Henry, knowing Jason's penchant for speed, proactively made the call to Canadian Air Force Command and alerted them regarding the imminent fly-over of the high-speed craft.

Jason's relationship with aircraft was complex. Many years before, his parents had perished in a helicopter crash in the Himalayas while documenting disappearing glaciers. Jason's mother, Lizette, was alarmed that the ice fields of the Tibetan Plateau were melting twice as fast as glaciers elsewhere. The Himalayan snows fed the Mekong, Yangtze and Ganges Rivers—rivers that supplied life-giving water for two billion people who lived downstream. This water supply is often described as "Asia's freshwater bank account."

Scientists warned that only a decade or two remained before the annual allotment of precious frozen liquid would cease.

Lizette was determined to spearhead an international effort to assist the affected people in the region to prepare for what was coming.

Lizette taught Jason about the importance of helping others. She would explain how people all over the world struggled, often futilely, to protect their watersheds and forests from indiscriminate dam building and illegal logging. From his mother, Jason heard many heartbreaking tales, and as a result, his understanding of the world was far different than most children his age.

Jason's father, Malcolm Henry, was an active, public spokesperson for Lizette's work. Malcolm and Lizette had been very much in love. Malcolm deeply understood Lizette, and throughout their lives he supported her in family conflicts. But there was always tension: Malcolm and his brother Garrett were constantly at odds about how best to utilize their financial resources. Malcolm would voice his frustration about how the poorest and most affected by climate change were routinely excluded from the corporate boardrooms that decided their fate, but Garrett would have none of it. It was clear the brothers were headed for a showdown.

After the tragic loss of his parents at age 13, his uncle, Garrett Henry, had raised him. As Jason grew older, his uncle insisted that Jason attend the world's finest business schools. To distract from his grief, Jason immersed himself in the typical rich boy's life of sensory excess, but occasionally, often when he was daydreaming, an inner voice would hint to him that he had a special destiny to pursue. More clarity on the issue, though, always eluded him.

As expected, Jason joined the network of bankers, hedge-fund cowboys and real-life monopoly masterminds that had enabled the cabal to capture most of the planet's economic assets. His uncle soon involved Jason in decision-making at the highest levels. Seeking a diversion from his substantial financial responsibilities, Jason decided to take flying lessons at age twenty-eight. When it was clear Jason was passionate about flying, his uncle had ordered the construction of the ARV-2500xi *Skysaber* as a special gift. However, the

Skysaber had been surreptitiously flown from its base in the Nevada desert and used to release the technology of Universal Energy to the world. This in turn, had forced Garrett Henry to offer $20 billion to ransom it back from Water Langenstein who had provided a safe refuge for the craft and its crew in the Midwest. When Jason finally took possession of the unusual craft less than a year ago, he sensed there was something very special about the ship—that it had some kind of unusual history that was yet to be discovered.

Sinking below the cloud layers in the Lake Albion Valley, Jason deftly piloted the silent craft towards the granite mountain where the underground city lay concealed. As he approached the camouflaged entrance, a broad panel of rock, soil, and vegetation dissolved in a burst of shimmering light to reveal a yawning, carved interior. As the *Skysaber* slipped inside, the mountain surface restored itself as if nothing had happened. Jason powered down the *Skysaber* and exited the craft. He took the elevator to the lobby of the facility and was driven to Garrett Henry's home some two miles away.

Over breakfast, Jason's uncle explained the assignment: "Use the 2500xi to transport a dozen new workers to Oceion 9. It's our newest platform located near the Samoan Islands. The workers there are a rather unusual mix of, well . . . life-forms. We've got regular *Homo sapiens*, photosynthesizers and hybrids all working together. And regarding Ariel Connelly—don't give her any special treatment, but give her enough scientific information to whet her appetite so she can become personally engaged. If she develops an interest in the project, I don't think she'll create trouble. Over time, she'll want to be part of the team."

Jason laughed, "What you're really telling me is that you want to bring her over to the dark side, right?"

"Something like that, yes." Garrett Henry stuffed a smile.

"But why her? Is she really that important?"

Garrett Henry grew serious, his voice lowered. "She's been working with Walter Langenstein. I will go to whatever lengths I must to thwart his philanthropic efforts."

"What's so harmful about that? You told me you donated $20 billion to his organization—the Climate Justice something or other."

Garrett's voice boomed with anger. "That's what I had to pay to get the 2500xi back for you, protect all that advanced technology, and recover a half-dozen photosynthesizer escapees from Subcomplex 56. But that's not the worst of it: His operations directly oppose ours, and he's using my money to impede and delay our water privatization efforts. I've already ordered up an attack on his estate, and I intend to shut him down—and Ariel Connelly is going to help me do that."

"Okay, maybe she will, maybe not. But I haven't met her yet."

"She's cagey, so be careful. We need to exploit her naiveté. And be ruthless if the situation requires it. Get my drift?"

"Uh huh. How soon can I leave?"

"Supplies are being loaded into ship this afternoon. The workers and Ms. Connelly will board early tomorrow morning. Leave then."

CHAPTER THIRTEEN

At dawn, the holographic door of the mountain bluff dissolved and the *Skysaber* exited the interior hangar. Lifting silently into the sky, it executed a 45° turn and gained altitude over the Lake Albion Valley. Debbie Chen and the other photosynthesizers were up early and working in the valley orchards as the ship passed overhead. Debbie recognized the craft and whispered into the air as she tracked the *Skysaber*'s horizontal trajectory, "Ariel, I wonder if you're onboard. I do hope so. If so, good luck to you, fine woman . . ."

Onboard the *Skysaber*, Ariel found herself sitting in the passenger compartment with twenty or so Latino men and women. Mulling over the fact that she was again aboard the ship that she knew so well, Ariel recalled her travels to China with fellow photosynthesizers to build the first Universal Energy generators. But no Ewar or Jake at the controls this time. How she missed them. Just what am I doing here? she asked herself. I feel so alone. At the same time, her mind was burning with a million questions: Where was she going; what would she be doing; and what about the Spanish-speaking workers traveling with her?

During boarding, she had been introduced to the pilot: Jason Henry. Ariel found him compelling, yet distant. His thick black hair, two-day old beard and impeccable attire caught her attention. She liked that his eyes revealed solid focus and intensity; yet, she noted a kind of aloofness and sadness in his face. This caused her to wonder what he must be hiding behind his mask of strength.

Their first interaction was short and terse, but when she engaged her future mind, Ariel was flooded with images: confusing scenes of them together. She began to look for a way to better observe him. There is a story here, she concluded, and we are both in it as players. As her curiosity grew, she found herself spending less thinking about Catherine, Jake, Razr and the rest of the team who now seemed so far away.

Ariel decided to enter the flight deck to see if she could converse with Jason Henry. Stepping up to the viewing windows, she was just in time to observe the western coastline of Vancouver Island receding and the broad expanse of the blue-green Pacific Ocean filling the view to the horizon.

Jason glanced toward Ariel, intrigued by her ease of movement. "You seem quite at ease here. Most people are overwhelmed when they visit the flight deck—all the screens, graphic images and strange markings."

Ariel smiled as she walked along the bottom side of the viewing windows. "You might say I find this a familiar setting."

Jason was confused. "So you've been in a ship like this before?"

"Yes, in fact, this very one."

"How can that be?"

"It's a long story, but I have few questions for you first."

Jason failed to respond.

Ariel moved into the seat next to him. "Where are we headed and what's the mission? What can you tell me about it?"

Jason was enjoying the close proximity of this confident young woman, as his uncle said he would. Her presence next to him gave him an unusual sense of comfort. He also remembered his uncle's instruction to encourage Ariel's interest in the project.

With a sweep of his hand on the 3D control console, Jason placed the ship on autopilot and turned to Ariel. "Our destination is Oceion 9. It's a sea platform—an underwater facility where we're working to reduce ocean acidification. The platform is located in the Tropical Pacific Zone near the Samoan Islands."

"Why put it there?"

"The area has several still-intact underwater reefs and good marine biodiversity—at least what's left. It turns out that the rate of increase in carbon dioxide levels in the water is greater in this area of the ocean than the rate of increase in the atmosphere, so the acidification is more pronounced."

"And that acidification is making it more difficult for corals, calcifying phytoplankton and crustaceans to grow their shells. It's also messing up the metabolic processes of a whole range of marine organisms."

Jason raised his eyebrows. "You certainly know your water chemistry."

"I took some marine biology courses. But how can you reduce ocean acidification?"

"Our scientists have created a technology that strips excess hydrogen ions from the water. It's like a giant electromagnetic vacuum cleaner. That's why it's call the Oceion Project."

"Is this the only such facility?"

"No. There are eight others currently deployed, but this one is the newest. And de-acidification is not the only purpose for building them." Jason turned away and stared into the viewing area, watching the ocean's surface appear and disappear beneath the cloud layers above which they were flying. He considered how much information to reveal to Ariel and concluded he might as well be reasonably truthful—just to see how she would react.

"The platforms have multiple purposes. We agree with the more aggressive scientific consensus that predicts rising global temperatures will render large sections of the planet's interior land area uninhabitable by humans in a matter of decades . . . and many species will go extinct. So . . . where will humans go to survive?"

"Underground or in self-sufficient marine environments," said Ariel answering automatically, her mind connecting the dots.

"Now I understand." She choked on her words and fought back a rush of emotion.

Jason ignored her reaction. "Unless we slow the process of ocean acidification, we'll lose much of the sea life in the ocean."

"I know." Ariel swallowed hard.

Ariel's mind jumped to the obvious conclusion. "It's clear you believe that humanity hasn't much chance of surviving on the surface of the planet, so you've created these refuge centers—or whatever you call them—for whom? Just your friends? The general populace doesn't know anything about them."

Jason chose not to answer Ariel's question.

"So the bulk of humanity above-ground collapses in conflict and just withers away while the rich and their servants live some-what happily-ever-after in underground or underwater cities? Is that the plan?"

"Essentially, yes."

Ariel was speechless.

"Look. We have no choice if we want to remain a viable spe-cies. I know you and the other photosynthesizers have chosen a route to the future by altering your genetics to reduce your depen-dency on plants and animals for food. But I believe we can weather the oncoming changes in the refuge enclaves. Several are fully operational and others are under construction. The enclaves will enable people to wait out whatever wars, weather situations and who-knows-what-other apocalyptic events might occur until things resettle."

"And once again it's about money, isn't it? Those who are rich enough can make it to the other side."

Jason attempted to sound empathetic. "Look at it this way, Ariel . . . You've managed to get yourself into the inner circle—the select population that will survive the transition and build a new world. Isn't that something you might want?"

"It is, but I hadn't envisioned it happening quite *this* way." Tension was building in Ariel's chest as she attempted to process what she was hearing.

"You have the opportunity now to help shape the course of things."

"But why should I join your rogue, breakaway culture intended to serve only the 1% of the 1%"

"Because it's *your* future, really your only *viable* future. You have a whole lifetime ahead of you. That will not be true for most others who will struggle to survive on the outside when things really start to go south."

Jason paused, creating time for Ariel to reflect on his statements. His stare was penetrating. "So which future will you choose?"

CHAPTER FOURTEEN

Ariel was determined to rise above the hopelessness that threatened to drag her down into a black hole. The fact that massive
physical construction projects existed completely outside of the
public view and discussion was one thing. But the purpose of these
enclaves—to ensure that a select subset of the population would
prevail, while most others would likely perish in a convulsion
of violence, starvation and disease—was physically and morally
repulsive.

"We're coming up on Oceion 9," Jason announced in English
and Spanish. His voice was carried through the ship by the public
address system, alerting the passengers to prepare to disembark.
Ariel felt confused about Jason. She wasn't sure whether to consider him dangerous or perhaps merely a pawn in the Grand Plan.
Need more data, she said to herself.

Curious about Oceion 9, she made her way to the viewing windows. Originally a tiny, highly reflective speck in the vast ocean,
the floating platform grew larger as Jason began the approach.
The speck became a wide, circular, level area, with about half of
its surface covered with green vegetation. Small building units and
open space occupied the remaining top area. A transparent, arc-
like structure lay folded along the far side of the platform.

Jason explained the features she was observing: "The
greenery is an organic garden and the buildings house a

communication center, weather station and café. But what you see on the surface is only the tip of the iceberg—there are seven stories under the water. The top three levels below the surface contain an underwater observation area, cafeteria and lounge, transport hangar, housing and supplies. On the next four levels we have laboratories, air lock, energy generation, storage and electronics. Overall, its interior spaces comprise about 180,000 square feet."

The *Skysaber* descended rapidly. Ariel worried it was dropping too fast and too soon to reach the platform safely. Did Jason know what he was doing? He anticipated her concern: "We're not landing on top; we're going into an underwater hangar. I suggest you sit down, as there will be a jolt when we make contact with the water."

As the ship plunged into the five-foot-high waves, it shuddered and rocked, the impact pulling Ariel forward. Water rushed over the viewing windows. Although she had experienced a water landing once before in the *Skysaber*, this was not an experience she enjoyed. Still, Ariel knew the *Skysaber* could travel through underwater realms as easily as it moved through stratospheric spaces.

Once below the waves, the ship glided through the translucent waters. Staring ahead, Ariel was entranced by the huge, layered structure hanging motionless below the sea surface. Seven levels, each about eighteen-feet in height, gave the impression of an architect-designed, underwater condominium complex. Light beams descending from surface sunlight created a dazzling visual display. Ariel watched isolated swarms of multi-colored tropical fish circling around the structure. Occasionally, a single ray, a slowly cruising young shark or a grouper paddled lazily by, seemingly ignoring the human presence. Some sections of the elegant structure were full of windows, their interiors glowing with light, while other areas emanated steady streams of bubbles.

Jason honed in on a wide section of the structure whose exterior was equipped with red and green lights arranged in a rectangle. As he approached closer, a hangar door opened and Jason slipped the *Skysaber* into the underwater garage. The door closed behind them and water levels began dropping.

"Once the water is pumped out," Jason said to her as he began to rise in his seat, "we'll be able to unload."

"Nice landing."

"Thanks. I do this often. It's part of my job."

Jason grabbed a briefcase he had stashed next to his seat and prepared to exit the craft.

"Just what is your job?"

"My day job is handling financial operations in New York—our investments in energy and real estate, and buying and selling assets—commercial properties, mines, water utilities, doing land deals and banking trades—straightforward stuff like that."

"And not so straightforward stuff like creating a whole parallel world."

"Well, I'm not the creator, I just manage it. My uncle's the creator, I'm just along for the ride . . . and you should be too. It *is* going to be quite a ride."

A mental caution light blinked on and off in Ariel's mind. She wasn't sure what to make of it.

"It's time to go," Jason said, swinging the strap from his briefcase over one shoulder. "They'll be preparing lunch for us."

As soon as the *Skysaber* was docked and the workers had disembarked, Jason and Ariel made their way to the elevator. They traveled two floors to the surface and emerged into a bright, warm, sunny day. A mild wind was blowing in from the southeast and the muffled sound of small waves breaking against the sides of the structure blended with the voices of the workers on the top deck. Ariel shaded her eyes in response to the light. She was thrilled with the salty moistness of the air. Undulating azure water surrounded her and stretched to the horizon in 360 degrees. She was instantly aware that her skin was craving direct sunlight. "Yes, yes, yes," she said loudly to no one, stretching her arms out as if she had just met a best friend, not caring who was listening. She spun around with eyes closed, soaking up the life-giving warmth of the hot, radiant energy on her face. Jason observed her curiously.

As Ariel opened her eyes, she blinked several times, astonished to find herself staring at several buildings, an open, park-like area and green gardens—in the middle of the ocean. *Am I in a dream? This can't be real,* she mused. Such things only existed in science fiction magazines with articles about life in the future. But apparently the future was here—right where she was standing.

Still gazing out to sea, she followed Jason to a glass-walled building that overlooked the gardens. She asked, "I can't believe this place. Are they all like this?"

"Yes. Most have food growing operations and are about this size. Some, though, contain laboratories that are more focused on geo-engineering projects . . . like this one."

"How do you deal with storms?"

"We have a dome that's retracted right now. In foul weather it's raised to cover the entire above-ocean surface area. On the third deck below, we have a gyroscopic system that keeps everything nice and stable. If the weather is good, we can lift the entire thing out of the water and move it somewhere else."

"I can't believe that's standard equipment."

Jason smiled. "We have, shall we say, some 'advanced technology' and special expertise to draw from."

Ariel got the point and decided to take her chances with revealing what she knew. "You mean ET-sourced technology." She purposefully framed it as a statement rather than a question, just to see how Jason might react.

She was surprised he reacted so evenly. "So you know about that; my uncle said you were smart."

Ariel concluded Jason probably knew more about her than she suspected. She would need to be careful about what she said. "I've had some experience with the human hybrids."

"What did they tell you?"

"That there's been a long history of trading advanced technology for a free pass to conduct certain operations on earth."

"Something like that, yes. So what's been your experience with the hybrids?"

"Some of them seem to be open to sharing their knowledge with parties other than the military and its corporate partners."

Jason pondered Ariel's statement. "Interesting . . ." He wanted to hear more, but lunch was ready.

As they sat in the garden café overlooking the ocean, Ariel was full of questions. "Tell me about the gardens here? What are you growing and can you produce all the food you need?"

"Almost. It's a great climate. We desalinate the seawater and use hydroponics for growing salads and vegetables . . . and we've imported soil for fruit production. Protein comes from fish farms located alongside the underwater structure."

Ariel dove into the green salad that had arrived on her plate, served by a young man of Polynesian descent.

"Okay," she said, preparing herself to bring up a more difficult issue. "I'd like to know more about the refuge enclaves."

Jason took several more bites of food, taking time to formulate his response. "What do you want to know?" He averted his eyes from hers.

"Well . . . who decides who gets to live in these places?" Ariel was determined not to let Jason off the hook.

"I can't really say. That's not my area of responsibility. I do know there are lists, and a considerable amount of time and effort has been devoted to identifying the participants, designing and building the facilities and stocking up on supplies."

"What's the timeline for the collapse that you're expecting?"

Jason twisted in his chair and concentrated on his food. "That's the big question, isn't it? I don't think anyone, unless he or she is a really good psychic, can know for sure. We can only project."

A faint shudder rippled through Ariel, as she was reminded of her own psychic abilities and what she had seen of the future— a future without people. But now this made more sense to her: Perhaps she was viewing the surface of the planet a few decades hence. "Well then, what do you project?"

Jason inhaled slowly, not sure how to respond, knowing whatever he said would not be considered very positive. "During the Permian Age, some 250 million years ago, the temperature rose by 6°C, and 90 percent of the planet's species went extinct. Around sixty million years ago, some kind of quick carbon and methane loading of the atmosphere caused the temperature to rise by 5°C in only thirteen years. And some scientists say we could be looking at a 5 or 6°C increase in the next few decades."

Ariel listened patiently, not surprised with the timeline details.

"Humans have never existed on the planet under such conditions; we don't know what to expect."

"I know. Things could become untenable fast. So to answer your question—it's believed we need to have facilities and resources in place and ready very soon."

"But only the chosen few get to use the lifeboats . . . And you and your people get to do the choosing. Right?"

"Something like that. But we've already discussed this." Jason was becoming edgy and impatient.

Ariel turned away looking toward the rolling sea: Everything seemed so calm, so . . . normal, like everything was just fine; she couldn't believe they were discussing the end of most of human civilization within decades. *Decades.* It couldn't be. Whenever she thought about this scenario, she became depressed, and then she reflected on those lucky people born 100 years ago: They'd gotten the get-out-of-jail-free card, didn't have to ever think about climate change. Of course, they'd had their own version of horror—WWI and WWII—but until the atomic bomb became real, no one had to consider the potential demise of humanity, the possible extinction of the species. The threat of nuclear holocaust was terrifying enough, but at least it wasn't inevitable—like the havoc that climate change was now creating . . .

"Hey, let's change the subject," suggested Jason in a contrived voice. "This is not good lunchtime conversation. Could lead to indigestion." He forced a smile. "Let's get you settled. I think you'll find your work here quite rewarding and something to divert your thinking about such heavy matters."

Ariel eyed Jason warily. "What's the work?"

"Taking measurements of ocean health. You said you have some expertise in biology."

Marine Laboratory, Level 4
That afternoon

"I'll introduce you to the Director, and he'll explain the program to you. I'll warn you ahead of time, though, he's a bit unusual."

"A hybrid? No problem. I rather enjoy the company of these guys."

"Really?" Jason said, his voice indicating surprise. Ariel smiled inwardly, sensing she was knocking him off his game. He seemed so sure of everything, always needing to be in control and in charge of all the data. This time, she got ahead of him.

The laboratory had the high-tech appearance of the control bridge in the *Skysaber,* filled with copious touch screens and 3D control modules. A tall man appeared from behind a series of square metallic units about the size of a microwave oven. Panels on the units blinked with multi-colored LED lights and graphic display panels churned out a steady stream of numbers. He walked over to greet them. Ariel recognized him.

"Ariel, this is Zechn Reu. He's our Director of Water Sciences."

"Yes, we've met, actually."

Zechn Reu bowed his head toward Ariel. "Indeed we have."

Jason wasn't sure what to make of the situation.

"I thought you were a pilot," Ariel said to Zechn. "Now you're a marine researcher?"

"Zechn is an engineer," Jason said, "and besides building flying crafts, he also designed the de-acidification system and the Oceion sea-platforms."

"I'm impressed," said Ariel.

"Okay, then. Zechn, get her started on the data monitoring. I'm told we're a few days behind because of the unusual tidal activity."

"We are, but it will be easy to catch up now that I've got some help."

Ariel scanned Zechn's physical appearance for similarities to Ewar, with whom she had developed a close relationship when they had traveled together to China. Ariel still had not recovered emotionally from Ewar's untimely departure—a kind of forced execution at their base of operations along the western shore of Lake Michigan. But she had overheard a conversation between her friend Jake Westerly and Zechn Reu in which Zechn had disclosed that Ewar was his cousin. So given the personal relationship, Ariel was inclined to explore deepening the connection with Zechn. It seemed like a fortuitous setup.

"I'll leave you two to get started," announced Jason as he left the room.

Arial perceived confusion in Jason's non-verbal behavior. She wondered what he was feeling.

"Come with me," Zechn said to Ariel. "I'll explain the project you'll be working on."

Ariel followed Zechn, silently noting the distinguishing features of what Ewar called 'blended human,' which generally meant ET father and human mother. Zechn moved gracefully, his arms a pale yellow color and his eyes were somewhat larger than normal, with darker pupils and less distinct irises.

"I understand you have a biology background. You probably know that although the damage to the ocean is not as immediately apparent as terrestrial destruction, it is indeed monumental."

"About 95 percent of the large predator fishes are gone, 85 percent of other important fish stocks are depleted, and there are hundreds of dead zones in the ocean where life simply cannot exist."

"Unfortunately, you're correct. But what we're studying here is ocean temperature rise and acidification. We see an increase in temperature even at depths below 1,500 feet occurring at a pace well beyond natural variation, and we're tracking de-oxygenation as well. All these chemistry changes are disrupting the food chain and the ability of a wide variety of marine species to survive. Have a look here."

Zechn opened a set of double doors and the two of them stepped into a spacious room dominated by a fifteen-foot high and thirty-foot wide curved glass wall that looked directly into the ocean around them. Light from the surface penetrated down far enough to illuminate small schools of fish that flitted back and forth, some disappearing into the darkness below. Ariel's attention was drawn to the play of light shafts that shimmered in the dark water like curtains in a strong wind.

"Do you notice what's missing?" Zechn asked, turning toward Ariel as the two of them stood before the wall of saltwater at a depth of 150 feet below the surface.

She thought for a minute. "It's kind of quiet out there. It doesn't look like what I used to see when my parents took me diving in the Caribbean, but that was a long time ago in shallow water on a reef."

"Shouldn't matter all that much. We're close to several large reefs that surround the nearby Samoan islands. That's why the platform is here—to study the changes in marine life as we run the de-acidification system." He paused and receiving no response, he continued, "It's too quiet, it's too empty. At this depth and proximity to reefs and islands, the water should be absolutely teeming with life. This particular area was once home to over 2,700 known marine species. We should be seeing an abundance of sharks, parrotfish, wrasse, grouper and hundreds of other fish varieties in massive schools coming at us from all directions. But they're just not here. The water is almost empty."

"It means the ocean is . . ." Ariel hesitated, fighting back a sudden wave of grief, "dying."

CHAPTER FIFTEEN

Ariel was determined to move beyond the frightening implications of Zechn's disturbing assessment. With renewed passion for preserving remaining ocean life, she lost herself in the microscopic world of plankton—the tiny and prolific marine inhabitants that serve as the foundation of the oceanic food chain and provide 60 to 70 percent of the oxygen in the atmosphere. Now she had the opportunity to observe them in samples extracted from the environment that surrounded her. With high-resolution microscopes and digital cameras, she found herself catapulted into their extraordinary aquatic world.

To her delight, Ariel's research had determined that the amount of ocean acidification in the immediate area around Oceion 9 was, in fact, lessening. A tiny speck of hope in a sea of despair. This was due to the effectiveness of the technology that Zechn had designed and installed on the platform. As he had explained it to her, a powerful toroidal generator was used to draw excess hydrogen ions from the water. The ions in an area up to several miles around the platform would be shunted through a collector mounted on the underwater platform. This reduced the formation of carbonic acid and allowed shell-building marine organisms to go about their business free from the harassment of excess CO_2 molecules.

Zechn had asked her to focus specifically on a type of zooplankton known as a *pteropod*, a kind of swimming mollusk or sea snail. The pteropod is popularly referred to as a sea butterfly. Because of its full-body transparency, Ariel could easily monitor its organs as well as its beating heart. She would spend long minutes staring into its shiny black eyes. Most captivating, though, was its ability to use its two feet as wings to propel itself through the water. She also knew it was not a good time to be a pteropod as they were mortally threatened by human activities—in particular CO_2-driven acidification.

Ariel quickly became transfixed by her work. She spent hours tracking the magnificent creatures as they made their way back and forth through her water samples. When backlit, they appeared as one of nature's finest works of art. One quiet afternoon inside the laboratory, Ariel dropped into a deep reverie. The simple beauty of these tiny organisms gliding through the water spoke to her of a kind of higher order that animates life. She began to sense a hidden harmony, in which everything had its unique place, and she knew she was a part of it—but what was *her* unique place and purpose in life?

Temporarily lost in reverie, Ariel flashed back to her solitary confinement in the underground city, to the moment when she spread the water on her arms and shoulders. She recalled her revelation—water absorbs and processes information, water is the connector, and it's water that binds everything together—all life and all time, and I am two-thirds water . . .

Then a painful loneliness began to arise—the loneliness of an ancient ocean emptying of life. And personal loneliness—those whom she loved were far away. She needed to reconnect with them, but how? Then it came to her—through the water—she could use the water.

Ariel hurried back to her quarters, a single room with a five-foot by six-foot window that held back the deep blue abyss of ocean. Below the window was a small table on which she had gathered grey, white, and orange seashells. Often, at night, Ariel would sit in candlelight, gazing into the sea around her, hoping to see signs of additional life in the void. She would try to imagine how, in the time long before she was born, this very section of ocean must have appeared when filled with an extravagant cornucopia of life-forms, thriving, competing and reproducing.

A bowl. She needed a container in which to place ocean water she had gathered that afternoon. She washed her fruit bowl and placed it on the small table. Next, she turned off the room lights, lit a candle and slowly poured her seawater into the black container. The candle's flame was reflected in the room's ocean window. Soon, its glowing luminescence attracted small clusters of swimming creatures, eager to satisfy their curiosity. Sitting quietly in a chair, Ariel observed the water in the bowl quivering, and she waited . . . It continued to vibrate as if expecting a response from her. She sensed the water was ready to receive.

Ariel took several deep breaths, releasing all thoughts of the day. Entering into a space of relaxation, she opened her mind. She thanked Water for bestowing the gift of primordial life to a ball of rock and creating the magnificent tapestry of color, determination, innovation, and astounding beauty called the Tree of Life.

Ariel reaffirmed her place in it all: that she and every other life-form were connected together by this miraculous and ancient substance. Then, into the mysterious memory fluid, Ariel placed her thoughts to Catherine: *I am safe in the far Pacific Ocean. I have access to information that could serve the greater cause. Please advise. Use the water as our communication medium. I love you.*

Having finished mentally projecting her thoughts into the container of water, Ariel opened her eyes to see a subtle pattern forming on the water's surface: Bits of light danced as she stared into the bowl, and slowly, very slowly, her mother's image began to take shape in the water: Catherine was standing on the deck of a sailing ship. She turned around startled—as if someone had called her name. Quickly, she found a place to sit. A rush of emotion flashed through her and she felt tears of joy forming in her eyes.

"Ariel, are you here?" she whispered into the air. She turned rapidly to scan the deck, but she saw no one. The message took form in Catherine's mind: *I am safe in the far Pacific Ocean. I have access to information that could serve the greater cause. Please advise.*

CHAPTER SIXTEEN

Lake Michigan
Aboard the sailing ship *Opportunity*

Catherine raced into the main cabin where the rest of the team had gathered for dinner. All conversation stopped as she burst into the room.

"Cath, what happened?" asked Jake, fearful something negative had just occurred.

"Please, everyone, sit down."

A dome of suspense hung over the group.

"I think I just received a message from Ariel."

"How?" asked Walter, trying to make sense out of her remark.

"I'm not really sure. It was like a faraway voice called to me. But I'm sure it was Ariel. It was not my imagination, I wasn't even thinking about her, I was just staring at the lake water . . . lost in thought."

"I think that's the key," exclaimed Razr.

"What's the key?" asked Walter.

"It's the water. I bet it had something to do with the water. You were in a highly receptive mode, right? Just letting yourself sort of trance-out over the water. Well, some indigenous cultures believe water can actually act like a big communication system to send and receive messages."

"Go on," encouraged Catherine.

"Ariel's got special mental abilities, right? We all know that. But she doesn't have much experience working with nature spirits or the natural world. She's still too . . . let's say . . . *nature-naïve*. Actually, that's something I would like to teach her about someday, and we did discuss that—her maybe going to Peru with me."

"Okay, okay," interrupted Jake. "Get to the point, Razr."

"I don't know what she's doing, but I suspect she's taught herself how to use water to communicate with you, after all, you *are* her mother. Water is the medium that carries us from the spirit world to the physical world, through women . . . Ariel must have somehow figured out how to use water to activate that connection with you."

Jake was becoming impatient. "So what was the message?"

"Something about 'serving the greater cause.' I think that's how she put it. Oh, and then she said 'please advise.'"

"Please advise?" repeated Walter. "That's a strange statement. What do we do with that?"

"That's easy," said Razr. "Ask her to try and get the information on those secret bank accounts."

"That's dangerous," said Catherine.

"I suppose it is," replied Razr, "but she *did* ask for our advice."

"That could potentially change everything . . ." offered Walter, speaking tentatively, knowing how this could expose Ariel to high levels of risk.

"I think it's a very scary proposition," argued Catherine, "besides, how would we get that suggestion back to her?"

"I can help with that," said Razr. "I know how to work with water."

Jake turned to Snapdragon. "Snap, you haven't said anything so far. What do you think?"

All eyes turned toward Snapdragon. "I suspect she's at a nexus of power. I don't know how she managed to get there, but she did. She gets lots of credit for that. She's up to something and is asking us for direction. Let's reach back to her."

All attention focused on Catherine. Catherine would need to make the final decision. Her mind was filled with memories and images: her pregnancy, Ariel's birth and childhood, their travels and tribulations together. The bond between mother and daughter felt stronger than ever despite Ariel's decision to make the leap to become a photosynthesizer. Catherine could see that Ariel was making her own decisions now, and Catherine had to, once again, let her go . . . to discover her destiny, whatever that might be, wherever that might lead.

The room continued to hold the silence, awaiting Catherine's response. The only sounds were the clinking of the sail and rigging on the main deck outside the lounge and the repetitive *brush, brush, brush* of the water against the boat's hull. A few gulls squawked in the distance.

"I'm willing to give it a go," said Catherine. "I hope I'm making the right decision." She turned to Razr. "So how do we do this?"

"I'll get some things ready. Let's meet back here in an hour."

An hour later

The group returned to the cabin to discover that Razr had placed a hand-woven bolt of cloth on a small table. A finely-carved glass bowl filled with water rested on top of the cloth. The bowl of water was surrounded by a circle of smooth stones gathered from the beaches of Lake Michigan. A single candle standing upright in the bowl of water provided the only illumination inside the now-darkened room.

Walter, Jake, Harrison, Snapdragon and Catherine gathered around the table, patiently awaiting Razr's instructions. Razr asked Catherine to stand facing the water. When she was in place, he started speaking. "I've drawn this water from the lake and passed it twice through our water purification system. The idea here is to return water to its purest state. That's our responsibility as humans—as we are the ones who have contaminated the waters of our world."

Razr then requested that everyone deepen their breathing and clear their minds of any distractions. Although they had never done this before as a group, they slipped easily into the process together.

Then Razr spoke, "We send our feelings of respect and reverence into the water and we remind ourselves that water is the substance that holds and nurtures all of life."

He paused and closed his eyes, as did most of the others in the room. The sound of waves washing against the ship's hull helped shift the group into a collective trance.

"Okay Catherine," Razr said, breaking the silence and handing the bowl of water to her. She grasped it lovingly with her hands. "Project your message into the water—speak to it."

Catherine was at first at a loss for words, but then her voice flowed, easy and strong. "Ariel, my courageous daughter. I've received your message. There is a great need for financial resources to relieve suffering and to right the balance on earth. We understand that you may be in a position to identify those resources. If you can help us access them, please do so, but do not endanger yourself. This is the consensus of the team. We send our love to you and wish you success and safety."

"Now take that water and return it to the lake," instructed Razr. "The lake water will transmit your message back to Ariel."

Silently, the group followed Catherine as she carried the container of water outside the cabin, stepped over to the edge of the ship's deck and emptied the bowl of water into the lake. The lake's gentle movements quickly absorbed the soft ripples of the splash.

In her black bowl filled with ocean water, Ariel observed a visual depiction of the ceremony onboard the *Opportunity*. Catherine's message reverberated inside her mind and a deeper sense of purpose began to arise.

CHAPTER SEVENTEEN

A red warning light on the wall inside Ariel's room pulsed rapidly while an alarm pierced the silence. The floor in her room heaved. Sensing an emergency, Ariel sprinted to the elevator and pressed the "Top Deck" button. She froze in shock when the elevator doors opened. The surface of the platform was awash with waves from a suddenly turbulent sea flooding wildly back and forth across the deck. Workers raced about, attempting to secure equipment and protect valuable materials from the maelstrom of driving wind and rain. A fierce tempest full of air-borne salt water lashed the exposed area. Despite the wind noise, a low rumble could be heard and Ariel detected the vibrations in her feet. She looked across the deck to see the protective dome beginning to lift into position. It rose slowly, fighting the opposing force of the wind.

Ariel's attention was drawn to a man urgently gesturing to her from the garden area. Ariel headed out into the rain, blinking repeatedly to clear the water from her eyes. The man was helping two people who were bleeding from head and body wounds. Next to them was a metal scaffolding that had collapsed in the wind. She recognized the man as Jason, who had a worker's arm wrapped around his shoulder. "Ariel, I need help!" he shouted.

Ariel could only nod, as she knew the wind noise would over-power her voice. Without a second thought, she rushed through the rain to assist Jason. As Jason half-walked, half-dragged the man across the deck, Ariel examined the woman for signs of broken bones. Finding none, Ariel concluded she was probably suffering from puncture wounds and shock. Ariel indicated with hand signals that she was ready to assist. Helping the woman to her feet and grasping her around the waist, Ariel moved both of them across the slippery deck, fighting against the increasing wind and torrential rain. Several times, as they started to lose their footing, Ariel was able to avoid falling by drawing upon her athletic balancing skills. Ariel's physical strength and confidence enabled the two women to make their way to safety, finally reaching the vestibule where an emergency clinic was now in operation.

Communicating with hand signals, Jason and Ariel headed back into the storm to search for more injured workers. Though totally waterlogged, with wet clothes clinging to her body, Ariel forced herself to ignore the increasing chill in her bones. Supercharged by adrenalin, she broke into a run to catch up with Jason. Just as she reached him, a towering wave plunged down on both of them. Jason lost his balance and was caught up in the turbulence of the water. The sound of metal tearing against metal rent the air. Ariel looked for the source of the sound, and to her horror saw that a metal communication pole had been loosened from its base by the force of the wave. It began falling toward Jason as he was struggling to get back on his feet. Ariel rushed forward, locked her legs, slid across the water-swept deck, grabbed Jason's flailing arm, and pulled him away in one continuous motion, just as the fifty-foot metal pole slammed onto the deck. The antenna and other equipment on the pole shattered into hundreds of pieces—wires splaying and components bouncing like loose tennis balls across the platform. Jason fell hard against Ariel as they collided with a large stack of sea grass that the gardeners had been using for compost.

Jason brushed Ariel's soggy copper hair away from her eyes. "Thank you—that was an extraordinarily skillful and creative rescue technique."

Ariel was floating in and out of consciousness. She struggled to remember what had just happened, and she was not quite sure what to make of the warm body that was pressed tightly against her. Appreciating the welcomed protection from the wind and sleet-like rain, she savored the moment of safety and security.

Stretching his arms around Ariel's back to create better support for both of them, Jason gazed upwards, grateful that they were shielded from the rain. The overhead dome was now halfway closed, protecting them from the full brunt of the storm. "Are you okay?" Jason asked, his face inches from hers.

Ariel wiped the dripping moisture from her face, feeling more settled.

"Uh, huh." she managed to say, striving to regain her internal balance.

"You just saved me from a fatal encounter with the communications pole. I owe you one."

Before she could respond, Jason said, "I see you're shivering. Let's get inside and find some dry clothes. The weather station is just above us. We'll check in with Zechn Reu. He'll know what's going on."

Warm and dry, Jason and Ariel entered the main observation room where Zechn Reu was hunched over a table that faced a water-streaked window. Ariel approached him and spoke what all three of them were noticing, "The sky is getting darker, like something worse is coming."

Zechn focused his cat-like eyes on Ariel's. "A low-pressure front is building very rapidly. With climate change, violent weather patterns can form faster than we can predict them. This storm is extremely powerful. I'm locking down the dome."

Ariel watched as he moved to a touch-screen control system on one side of the room. The building shuddered as hydraulic motors locked the transparent dome structure into place. It covered the buildings, gardens, and equipment remaining on the deck's surface.

A sudden rocking of the room caused Ariel to instinctively grasp the side of the table for support. The fierce rain and blowing salt water had rendered the dome opaque. Ariel's view of the out-side world was now completely blurred, giving her an unpleasant feeling of claustrophobia.

"Not being able to see out makes me very nervous," Ariel said.

"That's the disadvantage of the dome. It protects us but we lose visibility. We'll have to rely on our electronics or other means to see outside."

The words 'other means' caused Ariel to consider using her remote viewing. Why not? Before she could begin, Zechn Reu and Jason stepped over to a master console containing a set of monitoring screens that tracked the power, lighting and life-support systems in the platform. Ariel joined them and examined the graphics, which indicated that so far everything was still functioning. Feeling some small sense of relief, she closed her eyes and cast her mind outward to try and view the full extent of the violent weather. What she saw took her breath away—a massive spiral, a super-typhoon, was forming, full of lightning bolts and tornado-like water spouts. She started hyperventilating. In her mind, images appeared of red lights blinking on the console accompanied by an aerial view of the platform disintegrating. Ariel forced herself to open her eyes. Now everything looked normal again. Was she seeing a future event? How soon?

Feeling she needed to share her vision with Zechn Reu and Jason, Ariel said, "I'm receiving mental images that suggest this storm could destroy the platform."

Zechn was studying the multi-colored satellite weather visuals on his display screen. He answered slowly. "I'm inclined to believe you. This thing is growing much faster than anything I've ever seen, and the numbers I'm getting from it—pressures and wind speeds are off the scale."

Suddenly, the trio lost their balance as a hard force shoved the platform sideways and the room cracked with a sound like a gunshot. Zechn reached for the edge of the electronics rack to steady himself. Ariel and Jason grabbed the side of the table. "What's that?" Ariel asked, twisting her head around.

"Undersea earthquake—likely originating on the boundary between the Pacific and Australian plates. They create shock waves and tsunamis. Unfortunately, our stabilization mechanisms are not able to deal with very large ones. That's what we need to be worried about."

"Could there be more?"

"Yes, I've been tracking them. They've been increasing. I suspect they're due to the loss of glaciers in Greenland and Antarctica. As the ice melts and flows into the sea, the land rises, freed of the enormous weight of the ice. That, in turn, changes the dynamics of weight distribution on the planet's surface, and the earth's tectonic plates shift, which result in the undersea quakes. Because we're so close to the Pacific and Australian plate boundary, we're vulnerable."

A second shock ripped through the room. Lights flashed off and on and chairs slid sideways across the floor. A message on the console began to flash: "Alert: structural damage in Subsection C, D and E. Forty percent loss of integrity."

"The seismograph just registered another earthquake," said Jason, glancing at the instrument mounted on the wall.

"And a big one," agreed Zechn, looking closely at the instrument's graph. "About 200 miles from here. That's going to generate a tidal wave that will cause considerable damage on the nearby islands."

Zechn walked over to the console, punched in some commands and continued to gaze gravely at the platform conditions display screen. "What does this mean for the platform?" Ariel asked with alarm.

"It means," Jason said, without taking his eyes off the console, "more hits like this will destroy the platform. We better evacuate immediately."

Jason turned to Zechn. "We've got to get everyone on the *Skysaber.* Don't know yet how much the hangar and air lock are damaged . . . I guess we'll find out when we get there."

As Zechn gathered papers from his desk, Jason issued a terse command to Ariel. "Let's go, but take no longer than ten minutes to return to your cabin and gather up your gear. Meet me in the hangar deck—Level 2. And hurry, your life depends on it."

Alarms blared warnings throughout the platform, as successive shocks rocked it violently. Ariel found herself ricocheting from one wall to the other as she worked her way through the hallways. The elevator was filled with workers nervously clutching their bags and each other, their faces compressed with tension. Realizing she was descending further underwater added to Ariel's distress. Reaching her level, Ariel rushed into her room and stuffed her notebook and a few dry clothes into her daypack. At the last minute, she fetched the candle and the bowl on her table, pouring the bowl's water onto the already wet floor. Bounding out of the room, she lunged up the stairway up to Level 2 where the *Skysaber* was waiting.

People were rushing into the hangar. Jason stood beside the ship, assisting the workers up the stairs. Ariel watched water surging into the hangar from a break in the air-lock wall. The invasive seawater quickly morphed into a two-foot-high wave that was headed toward the line of people attempting to board the *Skysaber*. The platform rocked again and water rolled back toward the wall. It began to surge forward again, this time with additional accumulated water. Soon, the hangar itself would be flooded.

"Move, move, move!" ordered Jason, pointing his arms in the direction of the loading stairs. "Everyone get onboard, *now!*"

Another deafening, cracking sound. People screamed in fear and the lighting failed. Those entering the ship began pushing against each other in confusion. Jason reached to his belt pack, removed a powerful flashlight and turned it on. The pushing stopped. Jason shouted into the craft, "Zechn, turn on the ship's lights, we've lost power on the platform."

The platform tilted again as a four-foot-deep wall of water came rushing toward the *Skysaber*. People clung to each other in tight groups. Jason yelled in Spanish, then English, "Big wave coming! Hold on!"

The warning gave people just enough time to grasp the railing and each other. The wave surged past them, soaking everyone to the waist. A man came running across the floor followed by two more men and a woman. "This is everyone," he said to Jason.

Seawater had now covered the hangar floor and was rising fast. Once all the workers and crew were inside, Jason hit the red button that closed the hatch. It snapped shut with a comforting thud. Water from the closed hatch dripped inside the cabin, creating pools on the floor. The *Skysaber* rocked back and forth as more water began to rush through the hangar. Ariel made her way to the control bridge, desperate to know how they would escape. If the external air-lock door malfunctioned, they would become trapped inside the platform. Staring out the observation window, she watched with growing agitation as water filled the space around them. They would soon be totally immersed.

Ariel seated herself next to Zechn. Being careful not to interrupt his concentration on the ship's control system, she had to ask, "How are we going to get out of here? It seems the platform's main power's down."

"I'm activating the external door now. It's got an independent power system, just for emergencies like this. Let's hope it still works."

"And if it doesn't?"

"Then we'll have to blast our way out." Zechn pressed a button and then announced over the public audio system in both English and Spanish that everyone should prepare for a rough exit. "Find a seat. Otherwise sit on the floor. Grab onto something solid."

Ariel tried to relax as she felt the power build in the ship. In the background she could hear the fearful voices of the workers, tightly packed into a space designed for twenty. Some were crying, some were praying.

Bright lights from the *Skysaber* now illuminated the large exit door in front of them. Fish could be seen swimming in the water accompanied by debris broken off from the platform's interior. The water around them was slowly turning into a floating mass of rubble. Ariel was glad she had already experienced the *Skysaber* in underwater mode. She understood how her fellow passengers might be terrified, not knowing how the *Skysaber* functioned when underwater.

The exit door started to open but halted mid-way. Zechn repeatedly activated a command on his keyboard. "Must have jammed. Time to go to Plan B," he whispered under his breath. The *Skysaber* emitted a blast of photon energy that instantly illuminated the interior of the platform. The exit door vaporized and the water cascaded inwards at high velocity, driven by the pressure of eight atmospheres. At the same time the *Skysaber* charged forward, smashing through the incoming waves and remnants of the air-lock door. With a burst of power, it thrust itself out beyond the collapsing platform and into the turbulent ocean. Zechn turned the ship sharply upwards and in seconds the water released its tight grasp on the craft. Ariel watched the windows suddenly clear of liquid and fill with an expanse of wind-wracked, rain-sotted sky.

They were free.

CHAPTER EIGHTEEN

She waited until everyone else had left the bridge. Fighting back hunger pangs, Ariel decided it was more important to use the time to talk with Zechn Reu. She moved into the co-pilots seat. "Okay if I sit with you?"

"Of course," Zechn answered in his formal but friendly style.

"Where to next?"

"We're headed back to the Lake Albion Valley. Those are my flight instructions."

"Back to captivity . . ."

"How do you feel about that?"

"Remember when I boarded the transport ship in Nevada and I asked you what was to become of us?"

"Yes."

"You said something about a plan and that you knew of allies who could not reveal themselves as yet. Can you tell me more about that? I have a much better understanding now of this breakaway culture."

"You really want to know? You might not like what I tell you."

"I can take it. I've seen massive amounts of deception everywhere. I'm experiencing it first-hand. I see people being kidnapped to serve a privileged few, and I look at what's going on in the world: mindless environmental destruction, massive waves of economic and climate refugees, corrupt governments, and endless warfare. Then there's this small elite just sucking up all the money. They're busy building underground and underwater cities in an attempt to escape a global calamity—which, really, is the result of their own insane decision to exhaust the resources of the planet and enrich themselves. Why are we letting this happen?"

Zechn settled back in his seat. Ariel felt a calming energy radiating from him, and she relaxed.

"As someone who's half-human and half-something-else not originally from this planet, I have a unique perspective on the human condition. I see it like this: Humans are like lost beings; they're like robots marching through lives seemingly predetermined by their mythologies, their cultures, and their psychological stories. Look at human history: It's all about certain groups seeking power and control while instilling fear and insecurity into the Human OS or Operating System. This is what you've been conditioned to believe. This mindset has resulted in the squandering of vast amounts of natural resources and valuable human capital in senseless wars."

"But why do this? Humans can do better."

"Of course they can. But I observe that most humans are far too distracted by trivialities. And unfortunately, there are forces at work—with great influence, money and political power, operating behind the scenes with no oversight, that have far more influence on people's lives than they know or would care to know."

Ariel was not sure how to relate to to Zechn's statement. It raised troubling questions. "I've heard this has been going on for a while—involving secret military and corporate groups. But what about the ETs, what's their interest?"

Zechn laughed. "Simple. Earth is a truly extraordinary planet. It's not just the often tragic, sometimes heroic, and generally confounding behavior of humans that draws the attention of others, but also the planet's natural resources and the spectacular biodiversity and richness of life-forms—the result of billions of years of evolution. Take, for example, the captivating melodies of songbirds or the exuberant expressions of color, design, and fragrance in flowers; the complex and hidden lives of forest, air and ocean dwellers. Sadly, human activity is diminishing this evolutionary bounty at a ferocious pace. It's something that's profoundly troubling to many ETs."

"I care deeply about these things, too. I want to see life preserved, not destroyed—that's why I'm here. I'm willing to speak out and take risks to determine what's true and what's real. But it's so hard to know the truth, given all the misinformation from the media and the secret agendas of governments . . . and the wild-card factor of ET influences you're describing. I can get so discouraged because it seems to me that what most people and governments talk about is so detached from what really matters."

"What do you think really matters?"

"I think we need to find a way to move beyond the fear-based and separate-from-everything reality that we live in most of the time. We need to move beyond the distracted, dumbed-down way of living that seems to be the norm. If you're calling it an operating system, then I'm calling it a deeply flawed operating system."

"Do you think it can be changed?"

"I don't know, but I want to try. I think we need to create Human 3.0. That's why I decided to modify my genetics and become a photosynthesizer. That's where I . . . and we . . . those who are willing . . . need to go."

"Yes. Human 2.0—*Homo sapiens*—appears incapable of attaining the level of collective maturity that would ensure its long-term survival."

"If that's really the case, then, how do you suggest we could create the conditions for humans to truly thrive?"

"Actually, it's rather simple: You already know the answer. It's living in the present and learning to connect with each other and with all of life."

Ariel's eyes sparkled with understanding. "Ever since I decided to become a photosynthesizer, I've been receiving faint messages from the algae. I find I'm being reminded that I, as a human, am related *physically* to a life-form that prevailed and prospered on this planet for billions of years despite multiple extinction events. Because of my decision to share genes with this species, it's part of me now . . . and so I feel myself to be an integral part of a much larger universe. When I take the time to quiet my mind, I feel at peace. It's wonderful."

Zechn replied knowingly, "Welcome to Human 3.0."

CHAPTER NINETEEN

The *Skysaber* zigged and zagged its way through the massive, growling thunderheads, dodging lightning bolts that illuminated the atmosphere like powerful strobe lights. The ship rocked unpredictably as it was impacted by wind shears and pressure fronts from the gargantuan storm. Zechn skillfully piloted the craft upwards, attempting to rise safely beyond the storm's high-voltage tentacles. Finally gaining enough altitude, they looked down on a massive, salt-white spiral that nearly filled their view of the Pacific Ocean.

"Damn," exclaimed Jason, who had just arrived on the bridge. "This is a monster weather event—a typhoon on steroids. The damage will be catastrophic for anyone living on those islands."

Ariel was thankful to be observing the storm from above rather than below. Yet, she felt a wave of compassion for the people whom she expected would lose loved ones, livelihoods, homes, and perhaps their own lives as well due to nature's supercharged wrath. She reflected: Water is now doing the killing. Water gives life but it also takes life away. Was this nature's way of sending a message to humanity? Has humanity pushed the atmosphere and the oceans so far out of kilter that nature was just doing what needs to be done to return things to equilibrium?

Still, she thought, the unfolding calamity will be hardest on the poor. That was what troubled her the most.

Ariel approached Jason who was examining a large 3D image of the typhoon on a screen with Zechn. "I need to know where you're taking me."

Jason responded brusquely, "I had originally planned to drop you and everyone else at one of the other Oceion platforms, but I've gotten word that everything in the Pacific will be out of commission for a while. Plus, we have injured people here, so I've decided to take us all back to Lake Albion Valley."

"Then what?"

"Our passengers will go back to their jobs in the mountain."

"And me?"

Jason fidgeted and found Ariel's intense gaze impossible to avoid. "I don't know yet."

"Am I to be held as your prisoner?"

"No, no, no," Jason said, shifting nervously. "Not really."

"What do you mean, not really? Be more specific."

Jason looked away. "I have a dilemma: My uncle directed me to whisk you away to the most distant place possible, I guess because he wanted you to be safe."

"I was pretty safe back in British Columbia. Why ship me out to the middle of the Pacific Ocean? And what kind of danger was I in anyway?"

"I don't know the reason, he didn't share that with me. I just follow his directions. It's always been like that."

"So what's the dilemma?"

"My uncle will not be pleased if he knows you're back in the valley. I'll need to keep your presence there off the radar."

"But he'll likely ask about me. What will you tell him?"

"To tell you the truth, I've not figured that out yet. Any suggestions?"

"Nope. But right now a warm, dry living space on a mountain top sounds much better than trying to survive on a mid-ocean platform that's about to be demolished into a million pieces by a giant tsunami."

Six hours later

Approaching the coast of British Columbia, the *Skysaber* descended into clear weather. It drifted through the twilight over the city of Vancouver. The peacefulness of the area contrasted dramatically with the storm that was presently flogging the far Pacific. Ten minutes later the dark triangle slowed its pace and sailed gracefully over the broad Lake Albion Valley. Aimed at the wide rectangular opening in the mountainside, the *Skysaber* slipped silently into its hangar. Once settled above the concrete floor, the hatch opened and forty or so passengers disembarked, several on stretchers carried by their companions. A medical team awaited the wounded.

Ariel gathered up her pack and walked with Jason to an exit door that led to a tube-like shuttle vehicle. He entered commands into the control module, and with a gentle swoosh they rode together through the tunnel. The shuttle halted at a small station sited in an outside parking lot. Ariel clutched her jacket close to protect herself from a freezing wind. They loaded their packs into the rear of a Cadillac Esplanade SUV. Thirty minutes later, she found herself sorting out her minimal belongings in a luxurious room overlooking the fall-browned valley. The night was dark and silent with just a few lights glowing in the distance, indicating the sparseness of the settlements below. Drained from the harrowing events of the past two days, Ariel collapsed in exhaustion and fell into a welcomed, dreamless sleep.

The next morning

Jason had asked Ariel to lay low for safety and not to communicate with anyone. He promised to return by dinnertime. This gave Ariel the day to re-evaluate her situation and priorities.

Jason returned in the late afternoon carrying several shopping bags. "I'll make us some dinner and we can debrief." He lit a warming fire in the hearth and disappeared into the kitchen. The house soon filled with the aroma of wood smoke and hearty stew.

During dinner, conversation flowed easily as they discussed Ariel's decision to become a photosynthesizer and their narrow escape from Oceion 9. Inspired by the golden flames that cast dancing shadows on the walls, Ariel sensed it was time to probe more deeply. "I'm wondering: Just what is the long-term purpose of this whole endeavor—the gardens in the valley, the underground cities and the ocean research platforms? I know it's about creating a refuge for a select few, to supposedly reconfigure humanity after it all turns to shit . . . but what happens after that? Wouldn't it just be more of the same, but a worse version? Seems like a throwback to me, not a step forward for humankind."

Ariel could tell Jason wasn't expecting such a serious question. He turned his attention to the fire and away from her. "Maybe we can transcend human suffering and ignorance, maybe even mortality. That's the idea."

"How is that possible?"

"By utilizing technology and artificial intelligence. We could reach a point where robots and computers have the capability of a human brain—machines with emotions, creativity, judgment, everything. You know—Transhumanism . . . Singularity."

"So you think this would be an improvement?'"

"Of course—man and machine, working together as a seamless whole. The machine can make its own decisions and actually improve upon itself. And then—no need to deal with sickness, confusion, or error. A perfect being, possibly."

Secretly, Ariel was in turmoil. This was the opposite of the world she hoped to inhabit. She was thinking: Rather than 'man and machine' it should be 'humans and nature.' And this sounded like a warped gender thing—men thinking they could create 'a perfect being' on their own. Suddenly feeling a terrible weight on her shoulders, Ariel realized she had to find a way to put a crack in the wall.

"An ambitious goal, but do you really think it's possible to devise a computer or an artificial means to encapsulate the fullness of the human mind and the richness of human consciousness? Sounds like a fools errand to me."

"It's a lot, granted, but think of the benefits."

"Benefits? There's a huge risk here. I would fear a runaway effect where the machine decides to go its own way and take control—maybe even ending human civilization in an event that it would instigate."

Jason considered Ariel's worst-case example. "We'd need to put in place preventative measures."

"Yeah, right! History has plenty of examples where men's best efforts to prevent bad things from happening have failed miserably. This obsession with designing clones and smart robots is pretty weird and really scary. I don't think anything good will come of it."

Jason turned away. Ariel could see she was losing his attention. "Consider this: What if our technology is leading us *away* from the point of maximum benefit? That it's encouraging and promoting separation from a deeper, more rewarding experience of life."

"What do you mean?"

"For some, spending a day in an artificially programed reality may seem like a lot of fun and perhaps highly educational, but what if it's a program designed for deception and illusion? It could just as easily be propaganda and mind control. Or at the very least, a means to keep people so distracted they won't think about things that are *really* important."

"You have point there, it would depend on who's doing the programming."

"I think we should always question the intention behind the message."

"So what's a better alternative? Is there one?"

Ariel stared into the fire. She sensed Jason's curiosity. "Yes, there is: It's about sharing your hopes and dreams and your successes and failures with others. Asking questions about the purpose of life—sharing what's truly meaningful to you and listening to what's important to them. And spending days, weeks and months in nature—what's left of it—without a mobile phone or an Internet connection. You might discover things you never before imagined."

Jason was silent. Ariel could tell his deeper mind was taking in her statements. His gaze shifted focus to somewhere in the distance and his blue eyes moistened.

"Have you ever wondered how it might feel to help those people who need it the most?"

Lost and gazing into the flames, Jason's voice filled with a distant sadness. "That's what my mother's life was all about. She cared about helping people . . . that's what she was doing when she died."

"I'm sorry Jason. I didn't know . . . Can you tell me more?"

"Lizette was her name. She was born to a farm family in the south of France. Her grandfather was a French resistance fighter in WWII. Her father was active in world relief organizations, and that's what sparked her passion. She wanted a relevant education, so she enrolled in the School of International and Public Affairs at Columbia University. That's where she met my dad who was attending a seminar in global economic policy. They fell in love, got married and moved to Paris. But the family stuff was hard. My dad felt very connected to my mom's family in France. He told me that's where we belonged. But my mom hated attending the Henry family functions. Huge clash in values. My dad was always defending her against his brother's relentless criticisms."

"Criticisms about her work?"

"Yeah. She founded the Glacier Transition Alliance and Dad bankrolled it. They operated a fleet of helicopters to measure the loss of snowmelt in the glaciers of South America and Asia. They helped create water conservation programs for the mountain villages. I loved it when she'd tell me stories about the people in those villages. She'd describe how they followed the 'science of the ancestors'—building small dams and growing their crops."

"I wish I could have known her . . . And tell me more about your father."

"He was smart and sensitive, always reading, and always wanting to know what was really going on in the world. We hiked together and he taught me how to swim and made sure I could speak French and Spanish. And he wanted me to learn to fly. But then the crash—both of them and several team members went down during a sudden storm." Jason paused, his eyes filling with tears. "It took a major rescue operation to recover the bodies."

Ariel wanted to comfort Jason, wrap him in her arms, her empathic senses now turned up high, but she decided to remain neutral and avoid sending confusing signals.

"After a lot of court proceedings, I was sent to live with my uncle. But he has such a different view of the world. I was so confused. He condemns people who aren't focused on money and big business deals and he expected me to think like him. I felt I had to play along. It's been hard, but that's just how it is sometimes—you do what you need to do to survive."

Ariel spoke softly, "That's how most of the people in the world get through the day—just doing what they need to do to survive."

Fixated on the fire, Jason's mind was seeking solace. Ariel moved closer and placed her hand on his. She whispered, "You have the power to make a difference for millions, really billions, of people, Jason. You do."

"How?"

"Find a way to redirect some of the financial resources your uncle and his cadre of associates have amassed. Channel those resources toward helping people deal with the changes that are coming."

Jason continued to gaze into the fire without answering. It seemed as if he was in a trance.

He turned to face Ariel. "I can't imagine doing something like that."

Ariel decided to take a different tack. "Do you have any interest in carrying on your parent's relief work?"

Jason looked into the distance, as if searching for a lost object. "I often ask myself: Why me? How did I end up in a family with such astounding wealth and with parents who dedicated their lives to being of service? In my quiet moments—yes, I do wonder if someday I might be able to carry on their work."

CHAPTER TWENTY

Lake Michigan
Onboard the *Opportunity*

"Do you know if Ariel received your message?" Walter Langenstein asked Catherine. The tension at the dinner table was palpable.

"I've heard nothing."

"We can't wait. We need to move the program forward."

"What about the attack on your estate?" asked Jake. "Do we need to be concerned about more violence?"

"Most likely. We'll need to increase security. Obviously, we're considered a prime target by the Globechek hit team because of our work with the Universal Energy generators. They afford powerful options for self-sufficiency, as do our programs that help people gain more control over their local water resources. Then there's the information on advanced technologies that Ewar downloaded."

"Fortunately, Snapdragon made copies of everything," Harrison reminded him.

Walter continued, "They knew we had their spy in solitary confinement. Their special-ops team made sure they extracted him when they torched the buildings. I suspect they understood he had information that could compromise their operations."

"And I look forward to doing exactly that," said Snapdragon.

Harrison and Walter smiled with approval.

"The damage to my estate was not as bad as it could have been. The fire protection system saved much of the main structure. A large portion of it is still intact. We can still work from some of the buildings after the initial rehab is done this week. And it was a good thing we were in town."

"So you think the attack was meant to send a message to us rather than attempting an all-out assassination?" asked Jake.

"Can't know that for sure."

"And they may be back," warned Snapdragon. "Next time they may go for the kill."

Harrison shuddered and changed the subject. "It seems our adversaries are also attempting to sabotage the inner city garden programs by vandalizing our greenhouses and power generators."

"I'm not surprised," agreed Walter.

Harrison raised his voice, "This really angers me. They're disrupting our urban food production centers. I'm sensitive to the food thing. I've been thinking about this my whole life. That's why I decided to go the photosynthesizer route. The algae and plant-based production systems we've created are able to provide good, daily nutrition to people who really need it. We're helping hundreds of folks eat better and improve their health and quality of life. You should see the latest project we've built in the Adams Park neighborhood. When we're back in the city I'll give you all a tour."

Milwaukee
A week later

The residents of the Adams Park neighborhood had worked together for years to rehabilitate wood-frame duplex homes and nearby retail stores. The community had fallen on hard times since the freeway construction wiped out its core; the roads needed patching and several brick commercial buildings were boarded up awaiting future renovation. In the midst of the residential zone, a three-block area stood apart. As Harrison, Jake, Walter and Catherine approached the garden area, a small orchard, now laden with apples, welcomed them. In the middle of the orchard, a masterfully-carved wooden archway and gate invited passage into several acres of gardens flanked by large greenhouses. Colorful flags on thirty-foot flagpoles flapped in the wind above the main growing area. The landscape was full of muted autumn color.

Harrison led the group into the garden. "During the warmer months we grow vegetables and herbs in the open. In the colder weather, workers focus on operations inside the greenhouse."

Entering into the brightly-lit structure Harrison explained how they used compost to produce some amount of warmth but relied most heavily on the Universal Energy generators for heat, light and electricity. Thus, any destruction of the generators could seriously compromise their winter food production.

As the group gathered together in the first greenhouse, about 100-feet long by 40-feet wide, two young girls in brightly colored pants and shirts approached them. Their ornately braided hair was matched by their big smiles.

They jumped up and down with delight as Harrison greeted them. "Hi, Mr. Harrison, we knew you'd be back soon," one of the girls said shyly.

The girls stood by Harrison and examined the newcomers. He introduced them as Silvia and Natasha. "Girls, these are my friends. Tell them what you think of our gardens."

Each waited for the other to speak first. Natasha took the lead. "Healthy food is really important and so is taking care of our neighborhood."

"Can you tell us why we grow food here?" Harrison asked.

Silvia, now feeling more courageous, spoke up, "We grow our own food because much of the food in the stores is not very healthy. The kids in my class at school come here every week to work in the garden and get food. We really love the carrots."

Harrison addressed the group. "This is why a project like this is so essential for both growing healthy food and building community: Urban agriculture can bring people together and strengthen relationships while encouraging connection with nature. When we're in full production mode, you would see people of all ages working on rows of vegetables and salad greens. It's amazing when the school kids are here. They seem so happy, and their teachers say that afterwards, they focus better in class . . . Maybe it *is* the carrots!" Harrison chuckled. "Let's go next door."

Harrison led the group into a second greenhouse. It was filled with a shallow pond of dark green water. "Spirulina is our high-protein food source. Three hundred times more protein can be grown per acre with spirulina than with beef. We want to offer an alternative to industrial animal agriculture and factory farms because it's the leading cause of species extinction, greenhouse gas emissions and soil and water contamination. As we speak, millions are dying of starvation. The choices we make about food are, in fact, powerful environmental and political acts—that's how I see it."

"Impressive," said Walter. "And how many projects like this are we up to now?"

Harrison answered, "Maybe fifty of the urban food production programs are underway in cities around the Midwest—here in Milwaukee and also in Madison, Toledo, Toronto, Cleveland, Chicago, Detroit, Minneapolis . . .

"And there's more," said Harrison. "There's a whole educational component too."

Harrison led the group into an adjacent winterized two-story building. The ground floor was divided into open spaces and rooms. As the group walked through the building, Harrison continued as tour guide. "On this floor we have laboratories and classrooms where we work with school kids and also train our staff in science, managerial, marketing and accounting skills. We especially emphasize science skills. We also have a café that prepares and serves great spirulina, fruit and vegetable smoothies. Several businesses have been formed to distribute drinks and salad greens to local restaurants and retail supermarket outlets. But it's not just about food, it's also about life skills and *hope*."

"Hope?" asked Walter.

"Yep, hope," said Harrison. "When we first began our project, that's what the local elders told us they needed most. They said their young people 'had no hope.' Without hope, you have no future, and that sense of despair coupled with poverty can lead to anger and violence."

"And that's exactly why we need to share these projects with as many people as we can around the world . . . whom I suspect are also without hope," said Walter.

"Does the ACJC have enough resources to do that?"

"No," said Walter soberly. "Our current resources are woefully inadequate. That's why we need *a lot* more money. And it's not just about the food. Good land is needed, clean water and the right kind of equipment and tools—and relevant education. Everyone deserves some measure of stability and security. There's so much to consider when we're addressing the issues of poverty and lost hope, and that's why we're doing what we're doing. We *can* make a difference. Garrett Henry and his thugs will not stop us—that I promise you."

CHAPTER TWENTY ONE

Lake Albion Valley

Following a day of meetings with his uncle, Jason returned to his stone and timber lodge. He approached the solarium where he knew Ariel liked to spend the daylight hours, soaking up the sunlight to generate a portion of her nutritional requirements as a photosynthesizer.

With six hours of strong sunlight, Ariel needed only a few snacks and light meals to obtain all her daily energy. With glass on three sides, Jason's solarium was ready-made for a human photosynthesizer. The room included a lap pool, hot tub and an assortment of tropical plants. On the south side of the lodge was its most outstanding feature: the view. It included a fertile valley of vineyards, orchards and the sparkling Lake Albion.

Ariel was wrapped in a colorful robe, brushing her hair.

"I've just come from a meeting with my uncle. He's concerned about the trouble with our water projects in India. He's asked me to investigate."

"What's the problem?"

"Demonstrations, apparently. I'll need to take you with me. Are you game?"

"Yes. When do we go?"

"I need to make sure no one sees you. We'll leave before dawn."

The next morning

Jason and Ariel departed the house under cover of darkness, carrying minimal luggage. Jason drove the three miles to the underground base and together they took the shuttle to the hangar area. Jason loaded provisions into the craft, and soon the *Skysaber* was airborne in the dawn sky, heading north and east over Canada toward their destination: Nagpur, India.

Jason set the speed of the *Skysaber* to Mach 4 so they'd make the 7,140-mile journey in two-and-a-half hours. They were planning to spend the night in Nagpur as the guests of Globechek's Indian water company manager.

Ariel gazed through the viewing windows, lost in thought. As they transited the western border of China, she said to Jason, "Did you know that 300 million Chinese have no access to fresh water? That's because one-third of China's lakes, half of its rivers, and almost 90% of its urban groundwater supply is severely polluted. There are parts of China that have no flowering plants as the pollinators are gone, and the areas have suffered a complete biotic collapse."

Jason absorbed this shocking information with a silent grimace.

Approaching India, Ariel asked Jason to slow to commercial airline speed and swing low over the Bangladesh Delta. The flat green and brown delta was infused with countless rivulets of blue waterways leading back from the sea. It was easy to see how cyclones could rip across the wetlands and the fan-shaped coastline, which would offer no resistance to the assault of wind and water. Making matters worse, Bangladesh regularly suffered from the relentless cycle of intense monsoons followed by searing drought conditions.

"Have you ever thought about the relationship between people and water?" Ariel asked.

"No, not really. I just assume it's always there for us and it does its thing when needed."

"Consider this: When we're in the womb we're 98 percent water. When we're born, we're 90 percent water. By the time we're adults, we're down to maybe 65 percent, and when we die our water content is around 50 percent. Physically, we're mostly water. And water provides us with energy too."

"Energy?"

"Yes. Life energy. I believe the *energy* that water carries has a lot to do with determining our physical and mental health. Do you follow me?"

Jason reflected on Ariel's comments. "That's an interesting concept—water as energy. I can understand water as having *physical* energy. When water is boiled, it expands by 2,200 times. That's what makes a steam engine work."

"Well then, I guess we could say that water made the Industrial Revolution possible. That's not small stuff." Ariel's animation increased. "But I'm interested in the quality of energy that determines *life-force*. If water stores information and water becomes polluted, then polluted water will carry negative information. Truly clean water, on the other hand, like pristine water exposed to sunlight and twirling through myriad vortexes around rocks and down cliffs, would carry good energy. Such water, then, is more likely to support health and happiness in people."

Jason said nothing as he looked away.

Ariel was not deterred. "This is something I've come to understand: Water and life-force energy are intimately linked. It's water that transports energy throughout our bodies using our blood as the medium. Water is integral to cellular communication. Good water, good energy, good health. Bad water, bad energy, bad health."

"So are you blaming the water?"

"No, it's people who have polluted the water—all over the world. If we treat water as a sewer, no wonder the world is awash in chaos, chronic disease and suffering. If we could do something to change this relationship, I think we could begin to shift the world away from the global calamity that's unfolding."

Ariel stepped away from the viewing window, seeking privacy for her thoughts and emotions.

Jason placed the *Skysaber* on automatic pilot and joined Ariel. "Apparently, this is something you really care about. My parents cared about water, too."

As Ariel turned toward Jason, she looked straight ahead and her voice strengthened unexpectedly. "I see what's happening, and it's hard to take because I see what could be done."

"You're just one person—what can one person do about such huge problems?"

"Often I think 'not much,' but I believe that how humans relate to water will determine whether we and so many other life-forms will continue to exist. We need to seriously reexamine our relationship with water . . . and soon."

CHAPTER TWENTY TWO

Nagpur, India

Jason landed the *Skysaber* in a soccer field on an old British estate. As they exited the parked craft, Jason and Ariel were met by a man in his forties, smartly dressed in khaki slacks, beige shirt and white linen jacket. Alfred Morris was the Regional Director of the Globechek-financed New Asia Water Company operations in Central and Southern India. Noticing the quizzical expression on Alfred's face, Jason explained that Ariel was accompanying him as a water consultant. Her pale green complexion, he said, was due to a genetic experiment the company was undertaking.

"Excellent," Morris responded, turning to Ariel. "We have some serious local problems. Perhaps you can be of assistance."

Ariel smiled but offered no verbal response. She would wait and see what the New Asia Water Company was up to.

Early the next morning Alfred, Jason and Ariel met for breakfast in a sunroom overlooking several acres of manicured lawn and intricate stone walkways leading down to a well-maintained pond. Alfred was anxious to bring Jason up to date on the difficulties the company was facing with its water privatization program.

"As you probably know, the New Asia Water Company has recently acquired the water supply and treatment contracts for most Indian cities. We purchased the contracts from a French company that had become embroiled in corruption scandals and performance failures. We see a great opportunity in India, as most of India's surface and ground water is contaminated. India is well on its way to becoming the world's most populous nation, but no city in India has a comprehensive waste treatment system. And clean water is a very scarce commodity."

Ariel listened intently to Alfred, expecting him to talk more about the impacts of pollution, as she knew that many Indian children suffered from stunted growth. This resulted from the fact that polluted water reduced the body's ability to absorb essential calories and nutrients. The outcome was chronic malnutrition, even in children who received an adequate diet.

Instead, though, Alfred focused solely on the economic factors. "The potential here is huge because municipal governments favor public/private partnerships. The governments provide public financing, which means there's less capital we need to put up. Of course, we've had to appropriately incentivize our friends in important positions to make sure everything goes through the approval process in a timely fashion."

"So what are the problems my uncle seems so concerned about?" asked Jason.

"Nosey journalists and local activists. It seems they're always so critical of us. As you know, our intention is to supply clean water to urban and eventually *some* rural populations. We have the public subsidies for construction of the treatment plants, but once the basic infrastructure is in place, we have to get people used to paying for water. Of course, they love the convenience of having running water available most hours of the day. After a certain amount of time, we reduce government management workers on our staff, increase our administrative control over the system and increase the tariffs. We also charge the government management fees and they pay the energy bill. It's a good deal for us."

"What's the plan for supplying water to the outlying and rural areas?" Ariel asked, being careful to sound neutral, though she sensed the blatant exploitation apparent in Alfred's scenario.

"Water tankers. We've bought dozens of them. Later, we might introduce local water treatment and delivery infrastructure—if the revenue picture looks promising."

"And how about the city slum dwellers? Do they get the water too, and what's the cost for them?"

"We provide free water for an initial period of time, usually nine months. After that they need to pay."

"That's not very long, considering they're going to need it for a lifetime."

Alfred avoided looking directly at Ariel and continued to butter his toast. His voice sharpened. "We do not consider water a fundamental human right—it's a commodity. Water may be free at the source, the river or a lake, but it requires a major capital investment to buy pumps and pipes and chemicals and pay workers to build and manage a water system. If people want water, they'll have to pay for it—that's just the way it is."

"And the issue of nosey journalists and the activists? Tell me more about that," Jason asked.

In-between bites of his toast, Alfred continued, "Journalists like to excite the public by alleging corruption in government and conflict of interest between our people and the bureaucracies. They don't seem to understand that as a vendor we need to have close relationships with our clients, and people need to be paid for the services they perform. This is a public-private partnership. There has to be a *quid pro quo* for this to work. It's true: water costs will double and triple once the service is provided, but that's to be expected and that's when the activists get involved."

"I've been asked by my uncle to personally investigate the situation," said Jason. "Can you take us out to visit some of the problem areas?"

"Of course. I'll have a car ready as soon as we finish up here."

Inside the Nagpur slums

Jason and Ariel were not prepared for what they saw. The statistics say that Nagpur has approximately 500 slums housing more than nine million people, and most slum residents have no access to safe drinking water, decent housing, power, sanitation, roads, and proper drainage. Ariel walked along in silence as Jason and Alfred talked business. She noticed Jason seemed distracted. They worked their way down a noisy street choked with people and animals as un-muffled motorbikes rushed past tattered billboards. Masses of people crowded alleyways in an attempt to avoid the burning sunlight by squatting in the shade behind walls of deteriorating plywood, corrugated metal and plastic-tarped shacks.

They turned into an alleyway. Ariel gasped at the overwhelming odor of human and animal waste that permeated the air. While walking, she had to carefully avoid stepping into piles of garbage and other slippery matter that could easily cause her to fall into the open sewer of black water that flowed listlessly through the alley. In the water floated plastic bottles, pieces of dirty cloth, animal bones and human sewage. Ariel was shocked to see young children running barefoot through the alleyway, gingerly stepping around her and avoiding the shallow, watery canal.

Alfred pointed out where the water lines entered into the slum and admitted that the infrastructure was antiquated, so the company could not ensure that the water was safe to drink. He then led Jason and Ariel into a wide, open space filled with marching demonstrators—men dressed in white shirts and women in colorful saris. In rows of straight lines, they moved forward carrying a banner covered with Hindi script. Behind the demonstration leaders, dozens of men and women followed, thrusting hand-written signs on poles or sticks into the air. The crowd was chanting to protest the increase in water tariffs and demanding that the government provide them with potable water. Alfred translated the signs for Jason and Ariel: "Clean Water is a Human Right," "Stop Privatization," "New Asia Water Company Go Home," and "Hands Off Public Water."

A protester rushed up to Ariel and shoved a flyer into her hands. It described a community water organization working to help poor people get access to water. Its masthead featured the quote: "Water costs nothing for those with everything and everything for those with nothing."

As the marchers continued into the main streets, traffic was forced to stop while the police struggled to move the protestors into the alleyways to clear the main roads. The protestors increased the volume of their chanting, and several protesters began to engage in shoving matches with the police. Signs started collapsing to the ground, and people stumbled over each other. The anger level was fast approaching the point where violence seemed inevitable. As the voices of the protesters grew louder, Ariel asked Alfred to translate what they were saying.

He hesitated, but complied, "Water, water, water. It's our water. It's our life. Hands off our water."

The approaching crowd forced Alfred, Jason and Ariel to find safety inside a cracked and graffiti-covered alcove. "So you see what we're dealing with," Alfred said, frustrated. "It's been like this in just about every one of our project cities. It's maddening. We're just trying to help, but we've got to make a profit. We're a business, not a charity."

CHAPTER TWENTY THREE

Onboard the *Skysaber*
The next day

The Skysaber skimmed along at 80,000 feet on its way back to the United States. Ariel noticed that Jason appeared troubled. He sat down next to her. "To tell you the truth, I'm not comfortable with the water privatization projects. It's all about maximizing profit. There's little interest in making water available to those who least can afford it, and privatization often eliminates local input and ownership. I find myself relating more to the demonstrators."

Ariel gave Jason plenty of space to reflect. He continued, "Most of my family members go to great efforts and expense to insulate themselves from the sphere of human suffering, but what's really happening in the world is shocking. I'm not quite sure how to deal with it."

Ariel saw an opening. "Aren't you being trained to serve as a financial manager? Isn't that what you do in New York?"

"Yes."

This is the Big One, Ariel thought—just go for it. "Why not use some of those funds to help people get access to clean water? Maybe transfer some of those billions hidden in secret bank accounts."

"How do you know about that?"

Ariel tried to act casual. "Well, sometimes I can see things that aren't visible to others . . . But you know . . . it might afford a possibility of redemption."

"Redemption?"

"If we're to have any hope of creating a just world, the inequity issue needs to be addressed. It's gotten so out of balance—I've read that the 85 richest people own as much wealth as the poorest half of the worlds' population. That's crazy. Something needs to be done, otherwise things will only get worse."

Jason frowned. "Are you suggesting I take funds from the family or the corporate bank accounts and divert it to social causes?"

Jason turned away. "My uncle would be furious."

"He's the kind of person who *needs* redemption, he just doesn't know it yet."

"Yeah, right! I'd be disowned, cast out from the family, considered a traitor or worse."

"What if I could offer you membership in a new kind of family—a team of people who really *can* make life better for millions, not just create private enclaves for a select few? I would think that living underground with a bunch of selfish, rich people would become boring pretty fast, and I can tell you there will be revolution—against the enclaves and in the enclaves. There really is no escape. Maybe in space, I suppose—I've had those visions, but Mars is nowhere near as easy a planet to live on as Earth."

"Whoa, Ariel. You make a strong case."

"So will you help?"

Jason cleared his throat. "I don't know. What you're suggesting is pretty radical. I need some time to think about it. I'd catch more than hell."

Ariel stepped up close to Jason. "The times call for radical action. I'm just asking you to consider it."

Jason was non-committal. "I'll set a course for New York."

New York City

Jason slowed the *Skysaber* to airliner speed to allow for a smooth passage through the busy air traffic corridor over New York City. The tower at Teterboro Airport cleared him for landing at 5:12 PM. "Welcome back, buddy," the air traffic controller said to Jason over the comlink. "We've been missing you around here. We get a little bored with the standard executive jet. It's nice to see something completely different."

Moving toward his hangar at 20 mph, Jason took the *Skysaber* closer to the ground. By the time he was hovering over the tarmac, the hangar doors were sliding open. Jason brought the *Skysaber* inside and powered down the engine. Ariel was packed and ready to disembark.

Jason finished shutting down the craft's internal systems. "Okay, we're done here," he said to Ariel as he scanned the bridge for anything he needed to take with him or pack away for security reasons. Jason grabbed his briefcase and followed Ariel down the stairway ramp. She was first out, but let him lead the way once they had exited the ship. Their footsteps echoed inside the hollow metal hangar. They were alone, save for the two guards, one of which had brought Jason's Jaguar coupe around to the entrance door.

Ariel welcomed the fresh, cool air that rushed through the open door. Jason suggested she cover her face so as not to attract special attention from the security guards. She extracted a pair of sunglasses from her pack and concealed her skin with a woven scarf. She stepped outside. Ariel smiled as she inspected the salsa-red Jag, its deep, steady hum boasting of its 500-horsepower engine. The guard standing on the passenger side of the car opened the door for Ariel and she slipped into the plush seat quickly without looking at him. He offered to take her pack. "No thanks, I'll take care of it myself," she said, dragging it into the seat with her. For a moment she felt like a rock star.

The other guard held the driver's door open for Jason. "Thanks, Brad," Jason remarked as he moved himself easily into position. The door shut with a solid clunk. Jason shoved the Jag into drive and a leap of power pushed Ariel hard against the seat. The Jag left behind a trail of smoke and rubber on the pavement.

"Nice car," said Ariel, as she visually examined the car's luxury interior.

"It gets me around. It's not the best time to be traveling into the city. Normally we'd arrive downtown at the bank in about forty-five minutes, but we're going through rush hour so it'll take a little longer. Which is good. I want the place to be quiet when we get there."

It had been years since Ariel had visited New York City, so she savored the dramatic skyline as they crossed the George Washington Bridge and worked their way across town, then onto FDR Drive. An hour passed, as Ariel watched as the ribbons of cars, trucks and yellow taxis fought each other for road space. Finally free of the heaviest traffic, Jason turned the Jaguar into the Wall Street area. He slowed the car as they passed a towering silver and glass skyscraper. In front of the marble entrance steps stood a twenty-foot-high bronze sculpture of a man in a business suit holding a briefcase in one hand and a globe in the other. Burnished metal letters on the briefcase read *Terra absolutum dominium*. Four-foot-high, art-deco chrome lettering above the double-gilded-door-entrance-way spelled out "ARCBank." Seconds later, Jason slid the car into the underground parking garage. The tires squealed as the vehicle wheeled around the sharp turns, finally coming to rest in a reserved parking space next to a yellow elevator entrance.

As they exited the car, Jason said to Ariel, "It's well after six, so most of the staff should be gone. I've got a private entrance, but it's best if we're not noticed . . . especially you." He turned to Ariel.

"I'll be my invisible best," she replied.

"Hey. You're psychic, right? Can you scope out the elevator and the 60th floor to see who's up there?"

"I'll try."

Ariel closed her eyes, leaned against the concrete wall of the parking garage and shifted herself into remote viewing mode.

"There are people in the elevator and some kind of office party is wrapping up on the floor. I think it would be difficult to go unnoticed."

Jason thought for a minute. "Okay. We'll go downstairs."

Ariel followed Jason into the elevator. He pressed the BX Button, but the elevator failed to move. Jason opened his briefcase and extracted a plastic card from a hidden slot, swiped it through the card reader and they swiftly descended. The elevator doors opened into an alcove that led to a vault-door made of foot-thick metal. An electronic lock on its face glowed with LED lights and featured a card reader, keypad and display screen. Jason swiped his card in the reader. Next, he proceeded to enter a long string of numbers into the keypad. The display screen asked for a password, which he also entered. Ariel watched with intense curiosity.

The row of lights flashed several sequences and stopped. A loud click indicated the vault had unlocked. Jason turned a large bronze wheel, which caused the heavy door to swing open. As they stepped inside, Ariel gasped as the lights came on. The dark room suddenly exploded with yellow sparkle. She found herself staring at rows and rows of pallets of meticulously stacked gold bullion bricks, highly weathered, but still shiny in spots. Entranced, she stepped up to the nearest pallet for a closer look. To her astonishment, she recognized the stamp on the gold bars—an eagle suspended over a swastika inside a circle. She stared at it and ran her fingers lightly over the notorious emblem. Here it is, she thought, the symbol of unbelievable evil that led to incalculable loss of life and vast human suffering. She glared at the vile thing, breathless. Her head began to swim as she struggled to form the words—words she never in her wildest imagination thought she'd ever speak: "This is Nazi gold, isn't it?"

"It is," replied Jason, watching Ariel closely. "Recovered from tunnels in the mountains of Southern Germany."

"Why is it here?"

"For safe keeping and to secure loans and support the value of fiat money."

Jason walked into the space between the stacks of bullion. "There are some people who really like knowing they have access to huge amounts of gold. It's . . . something physical, a lot more real than paper dollars."

Ariel turned toward Jason, "Are you one of them?"

Jason laughed self-consciously. He lifted one of the heavy gold bars from the top of a nearby short stack and balanced it in his hand. "Of course I'm seduced by gold, who isn't? The stuff has such a powerful history and energy about it . . . And yes, it's led to untold tragedy over the ages. But you know—what we've been talking about during the past few days has me thinking hard about my life. How do I make sense out of the fact that such wealth exists here in the vaults below New York City while a billion or more people around the world try to scrape by on a dollar a day and are sick half their lives from drinking bad water?"

Jason replaced the gold bar on the pile.

Ariel looked around the room. "What all is down here?"

"Mostly gold and some jewels recovered after WWII from Europe and the Philippines."

"What's the story behind the Philippine gold?"

"It's the stuff of myth and legend. When the Japanese invaded Asia in WWII, they methodically looted thousands of years of accumulated treasure from the nations they occupied. They utilized slave labor, just like the Nazis, to excavate deep tunnels and storage caverns in the Philippines. The Nazis used underground spaces to store art and other valuables and also built factories for the manufacture of advanced weapons—like jet fighters and rockets. The Japanese, on the other hand, used their excavations mainly to hide looted treasure, and when they left, they sealed the workers inside the caverns. Much political and financial skullduggery occurred following the end of the war in connection with the treasure. It's quite a story. As it turned out, a large portion of the bullion ended up in the hands of the bankers, as is usually the case . . . So here it is."

Ariel found she couldn't take her eyes off the expanse of gold bricks that stood neatly in row after row, higher than her head and stretching into the distance. "How much is here?"

"Several banks in the city are storing gold. This is the largest stash. I'd say there's about 800 metric tons here, worth maybe $40 billion dollars."

"But gold is hard to convert into money, isn't it?"

"Yes. Flooding the market would reduce its value. The gold secures billions of dollars in loans from the banks, and the money is then invested in real estate, new technologies, manufacturing, business enterprises and various financial instruments. It's been used to generate huge fortunes."

"To provide financing for the breakaway civilization," whispered Ariel, turning around slowly and scanning the dark recesses of the cavernous, silent room. But the silence was abruptly broken by the heavy thump of footsteps in the corridor just outside the vault.

CHAPTER TWENTY FOUR

"Get behind the stacks!" Jason whispered as he pointed toward the piles of bullion.

Ariel jumped behind the pallets of yellow metal. Her hands again found their way to the sparkling gold. She felt the coldness crawling up her arm.

Jason casually walked toward the vault entrance. A guard in uniform was waiting for him as he approached the door. The man peered into the chamber. "Oh, Mr. Henry, I didn't see you come in. Is everything all right? I was just making my rounds for the night."

"Everything is fine, Matt, I'm glad to see you're checking on things. I was just doing inventory. We're planning to ship some of the material out in a few days to other banks, but I'm finished here. I'll close things up."

"I'll help you with the door," the guard said.

The two men shoved the heavy vault door into place. The massive piece of metal closed tight with a desolate, muffled *thunk*.

Jason and the guard entered the elevator and continued upwards into the building.

Ariel was once again alone in absolute darkness.

Her heart pounded. What now? Has Jason abandoned me? Left me to die in the dark among these appalling remnants of the Third Reich?

She slid her body to the floor and sat upright, organizing her thoughts. Light—let's get some light in here. She removed her jacket and rolled up her sleeves. Her exposed arms began to glow ever so slightly. In the pitch blackness her photosynthesizing skin generated just enough light to reveal the reflective stacks of gold bullion. Switching into remote viewing mode, she scanned the space around her in ever-widening circles, projecting her mind outward through the building. Compiling the data, her mind generated a sketchy view of her surroundings. Nothing seemed to be moving. She waited, relaxing her breathing, calming her nerves. He will come back, she assured herself. I know he will.

Ariel felt something passing by her face. A cool breeze? Air conditioning? No, it was already cold in here. More air movements. She closed her eyes, invoking her clairvoyant senses. When she reopened her eyes, faint black and white images were floating in the air between her and the bullion piles as if a film projector was mounted somewhere unseen, reeling off 3D movies from WWII.

Astonished, Ariel watched ethereal German troops marching in vast parades holding banners, with trucks and tanks driving alongside in carefully choreographed lines. Squadrons of angry warplanes soared overhead, as armies charged into Austria, Poland, and Russia, like so many ants on a mission. Bewildered Jewish families staggered through war-torn streets at gunpoint, clutching battered suitcases. Fighter aircraft jousted in the sky and bombs leveled buildings. Emaciated and exhausted men in drab clothes wielding shovels and pushing heavy carts full of soil, clawed at dirt and stone in dank, underground spaces. And faces: young and old, women, men, children—desperate, haggard, and weeping—futures terminated.

Ariel closed her eyes, sensing the room was full of distraught ghosts—phantoms still reliving that epic conflagration of death and destruction so many decades ago. She shook her head. This is not what she wanted to be thinking about. Inwardly a voice spoke to her: *Metal is matter. It too, can gather information and harbor memories, especially gold. Everything is connected.*

Ariel was losing track of time, losing her sense of where she was, losing her ability to determine what was real and what was fantasy. Her head was spinning—past, present and future tumbling into incoherence. She gasped for air. And then . . . the sound of metal against metal. The lights came on and the images evaporated, the agonized specters of the war-torn past had retreated into their other-dimensional lairs, flung back into their private purgatories.

Cautiously, Ariel stood up and peered out from her hiding place. A shadowy figure walked rapidly towards her. He gestured to her, indicating she should follow him. He raised a finger to his lips to ensure her silence. She understood and strode behind him through the vault door. Without speaking, she assisted him to close the door and seal the lock. As they entered the elevator, Jason kissed Ariel lightly on the forehead, as if to apologize for abandoning her to the darkness. She nodded with forgiveness.

The elevator ascended to the 60th floor. The elevator rolled open, revealing a single door labeled "J. Henry". Jason entered a code into the electronic lock. The door opened, revealing a spacious, comfortable room with a spectacular view of the layered and lighted multi-story buildings that surrounded them. In between the buildings, far in the distance, lay the dark empty spaces of the Atlantic Ocean.

Jason switched on a table lamp. "Sorry to have locked you in with the gold, but I had no choice. I had to make the guard think everything was normal."

Ariel was now beginning to relax. She faced Jason. "I understand; that was probably necessary."

Jason's demeanor registered guilt. "Were you afraid?"

"At first, yes. But I wasn't alone."

"What? How can that be?"

Ariel wasn't sure how much detail she should reveal. "It seems there's some . . . well, I'll call it . . . 'information residue' associated with those gold bars—old memories . . . very horrific."

"Can you be more specific?"

"Frightening images from the past. I was shown events that happened in relationship to the gold: the Nazi agenda and the brutality of war and what that metal funded."

Lost in thought, Jason walked toward the glass wall that filled the room with a light-studded view of the New York skyline. Ariel followed him. They stood together, watching the red and orange lights of vehicles moving against each other on the streets far below.

"I've had experiences like that when I go down there alone. Sometimes I just walk around those stacks of gold and wonder what tales they have to tell. And the history . . . It's full of pain, unbelievable pain. Sometimes I think I even hear voices."

"So maybe you're psychic too, but does anyone discuss it? Where it came from? Or that maybe that it should be returned to its rightful owners or their descendants?"

"No, it's way too touchy a subject. It's like a vice grip. The gold affords so much power to its possessors that nobody who has it would ever want to part with it. Like I said: It can seduce the best of us. It enables us to do things we know are often not in the best interests of humanity, but it seems we're powerless to do otherwise . . ."

Ariel softened her voice. "That doesn't always have to be the case. A strong person who knows what's right can chart a different course—and you could be that person."

Jason continued to gaze at the interplay of lights and high vertical buildings that filled the window. In the distant sky, pairs of lights strobed on and off, signaling the arrival of incoming aircraft approaching the airports around New York City. This was Jason's moment of decision.

"This way," he said to Ariel as he strode into the adjacent office. Jason fetched a chair for Ariel and fired up his desktop computer. Ariel positioned herself so she could also view the screen. When the display became active, Jason's fingers danced rapidly over the keyboard, entering codes and passwords. He moved quickly through the screens until the display became still, went blank and then began listing columns of numbers with dollar and Euro signs. It stopped after three pages.

He swiveled his chair to face Ariel. "How much do you think is needed?"

Ariel was caught off guard by Jason's quick actions. She struggled to engage her brain regarding numbers and translating them into dollars. Closing her eyes, she recalled the first mental recognition she had of the underground city in British Columbia. It scrolled by in her mind, followed by the raw scenes of hollow-eyed children walking barefoot through raw sewage in India. Those images then became overlaid by the ghosts of the gold in the vault and the power the gold represented to provide relief to the many and potential redemption to the few.

"How about a few trillion?" Ariel said, drawing upon her resolve.

"Jason continued staring at the screen. "How about fifteen? Can you work with that?"

Ariel's eyes began to water; she took a long inhale, and then she exhaled slowly, attempting to imagine what could be done with fifteen trillion U.S. dollars.

"Nice," she said, as understated and neutral as she could make her voice sound. Then Ariel realized that something far beyond wonderful had just happened. "This will make such a difference, Jason. Your parents would be so proud."

"Not so soon," he cautioned her as he returned his attention to the computer. He opened a desk drawer, removed a digital memory card, inserted it into the side of the computer and copied the pages of data to the card. That done, he removed the card and held it up to Ariel. "These are just account numbers. We still have to get the money out of the accounts. That's not going to be easy. There are major security protocols and firewalls in place. We'll need to find a very clever way to do this."

Ariel slid to the edge of her chair and placed a hand on Jason's shoulder to garner his attention. When his gaze met hers, she said with full confidence, "I know just the woman who can help us."

CHAPTER TWENTY FIVE

Lake Michigan, October

The morning sun was fast dissolving the thick fog that overlaid the water's rippled surface, revealing a ghostly shape that clarified into a triple-masted sailing ship thrusting its way free into clear air.

Jake stood watch on the observation deck of the *Opportunity*, squinting into the distance. A pair of binoculars hung loosely on his chest. Walter Langenstein was one level above Jake in the pilot's cabin manning the helm, keeping the ship on course as it plowed through the 40°F (4°C) waters at a 12-knot pace under full sail. As the weather cleared and visibility improved, Jake tracked an echelon of Canada geese flying overhead. What caught his attention though, was an odd bubble of distortion in the sky that visually erased a section of the formation of the flying geese. It seemed as if an object lay between Jake and the geese that was obscuring the birds from his view. Needing an independent confirmation of the phenomena, he reached for the all-weather phone affixed to the railing and summoned expert help, "I'm seeing some kind of visual thing above the ship; need your take on this."

Two minutes later Snapdragon was standing next to Jake who continued to examine the anomaly with his binoculars. "You see it?" Jake said, dropping his binoculars to his chest and pointing with his right arm as they both stared upwards. "Notice how it blocks out part of that formation. I'm sure something is up there."

Snapdragon knew exactly what she was seeing. "It's cloaked. Something is watching us."

"And it's coming closer. Friend or foe?"

"We better hope it's friend. We don't have anywhere to take cover."

Before either could comment further, the object revealed itself—a 110-foot-wide black triangular-shaped aircraft that hovered several hundred feet above the water and 150 yards from the starboard side of the *Opportunity*.

Jake was stunned. "I must be dreaming. It looks like the *Skysaber* is materializing in front of my eyes in the middle of Lake Michigan."

Snapdragon placed her hands on her hips. "This is way cool. I think I know who might be inside."

Walter, watching the events unfolding from the pilot's cabin, immediately alerted the crew and passengers. They swarmed to the fore and aft decks to observe the strange aircraft that lay suspended above the starboard waters.

Catherine joined Jake and Snapdragon at the railing. "It's the *Skysaber* . . . and it's just hanging there . . . like it wants to communicate with us."

Jake retrieved the communications phone. "Walter, heave to, bring us to a full stop. I think we're going to have some visitors."

Catherine was bursting with excitement. "Should I expect to see someone I know?"

Jake smiled in anticipation. "Possibly."

As Walter turned *Opportunity* into the wind, its speed slowed to a crawl and its raft of sails flapped noisily as they luffed, deprived of the wind. The black aircraft turned as well, descended to the water's surface and moved to within 50 yards of the sailing ship. Both ships now lay parallel to each other. Walter had given the helm to his first mate and was standing with Jake, Snapdragon and Catherine on the observation deck. Jake took the initiative. "Let's take the motor launch out to meet the ship. The waves are small enough that we could take passengers onboard. And look . . . the hatch has opened."

"Prepare the launch." Walter ordered the crew. Promptly, three crewmembers removed the canvas cover, unlocked the winch and lowered the boat, with Jake and Snapdragon onboard, into the water below. Jake positioned himself in the stern, his hand on the outboard electric motor control. Snapdragon settled herself in the front of the boat. As the crew and its passengers watched, the motor launch bucked through the waves toward the two-story triangular aircraft that lay imposingly in front of them, suspended six feet above the water. Jake skillfully circled the launch around the hovering craft, searching for the calmest waters to approach the deployed staircase. Water splashed against its lower steps. As Jake positioned the launch, two feet appeared on the top steps and an arm reached to the step's railing for support. Jake cut his power to the minimum in an effort to get as close to the stairway as possible. Catherine, on the deck of the *Opportunity*, had her binoculars trained on the stairway of the ship.

A woman appeared on the steps. Snapdragon began waving with both hands. "It's Ariel!"

Ariel waved back, a broad smile across her face.

Jake adroitly moved the motor launch next to the stairway, and Snapdragon threw a line to Ariel who attached it to the stairway's railing. Thus secured, it was now possible to transfer passengers to the launch. Ariel tossed her pack to Snapdragon who stowed it and assisted her in stepping into the bobbing boat. Jake smiled broadly and waved at Ariel as he kept his hand on the motor, moving it back and forth to keep the launch in a stable position.

"There's one more to come aboard," shouted Ariel.

A properly-dressed-for-sailing man stepped down, carrying a briefcase. Snapdragon reached out and grasped his free hand, assisting him to board the launch.

"Anyone else?" Jake asked the boarders. They both shook their heads in unison. Snapdragon grabbed the stair railing and released the line, and Jake pulled the launch back from the ship. The man in the boat then removed a device from his pocket, faced the aircraft, and watched as the stairway retracted itself back into the ship's hull. Once Jake was confident everyone was properly seated, he gunned the motor and returned his passengers to the side of the *Opportunity*.

Ariel and her companion were greeted with cheers as the launch was winched to the top deck of the *Opportunity*. Stepping onto the deck, Catherine embraced Ariel in a passionate hug as everyone applauded.

The man with Ariel was the first to speak. "Who's the Captain here?"

Walter stepped forward. "I am."

The unidentified man extended a hand in greeting. He spoke evenly. "Requesting permission to come aboard, Captain. My name is Jason Henry."

CHAPTER TWENTY SIX

Walter's mind froze as he shook Jason Henry's hand. Never did he expect to meet a relative of his nemesis, Garrett Henry, in the middle of Lake Michigan. What a surprise! This was a lot to process at the moment, but given Walter's practiced public demeanor, his internal autopilot saved the day. "Permission granted. Welcome aboard, Jason Henry."

Jason again retrieved the remote control device from his jacket pocket. Aiming it toward the dominant presence of the large black aircraft hanging motionless over the blue-grey waters, he commanded it to gently sink beneath the surface of the lake. "I think it's best no one else knows we're here."

As soon as everyone was settled into the dining area for lunch, numerous toasts celebrated the return of the prodigal daughter. The urgency that everyone felt for addressing the dire state of the world temporarily vanished, buried under the exhilaration of the moment. Soon, though, it was back to business—very serious business.

Walter asked his first mate to take control of the ship so he could focus his attention on the critical task at hand and provide the needed privacy. Ariel took the lead. "Jason is Garrett Henry's nephew. While we were in New York, he downloaded the account numbers that will give us access to certain financial resources. He's to be seriously commended. Without his help, this would not be happening and I certainly would not be here. Perhaps I owe him my life." Ariel turned toward Jason with a gaze of deep appreciation.

All eyes shifted to Jason. "And Ariel saved my life as well."

The room remained in awkward silence. Clearly there was a need for additional information. The rocking of the boat and the sounds of the rigging dominated the senses of the room's occupants.

"We'll do stories later," said Walter. "Right now we need to get down to business. What have we got here? What are we talking about . . . that is, in terms of . . . potential financial resources?"

"About fifteen trillion in U.S. dollars . . . I would estimate . . . is possible," said Jason, evenly.

Without thinking, Jake whistled.

Walter was momentarily speechless but responded formally, "That amount of money in the right hands and directed to the right places would have a *huge* impact. It could, in fact, change the entire face of the human presence on the planet."

"So how do we get it done?" asked Catherine, unable to restrain her excitement. "These resources need to be put to work immediately."

"Well," said Walter. "We need to ask the man with the money how that can be done."

All attention now focused on Jason. "We need to find a way to transfer the money without the Globecheck security system sensing multiple withdrawals."

"I can handle that," spoke up Snapdragon. "I have experience moving large amounts of money back and forth from secret accounts. Computers have, shall we say, *certain vulnerabilities*—just like people."

"What's the plan?" asked Walter. "How do we proceed?"

"This is what I suggest," said Snapdragon, exuding her usual sense of cool confidence. "I'll work out the transfer protocols with Jason's help. Then we set everything up to activate at a pre-determined time. But the money needs to go somewhere. Walter, what do you suggest? Who's going to receive all this largesse?"

"It will go to my hot list of NGOs, non-profit organizations and other worthy recipients. We'll immediately send a portion of the money to their accounts. I'll tell them it was an anonymous donation. I'll also set up a network of trusted private banks. They'll hold the remaining balance for later distribution. By the way, Jason, how will this impact the overall corpus of black-budget-money that I suspect is out there?"

Jason turned in his seat, apparently feeling some sense of personal guilt. He avoided direct eye contact with Walter. "This is about a third of it, I'd say. There's still a significant balance. But they'll miss it, I'm sure."

Walter laughed. "Yes, I'm sure there are people who would miss $15 trillion suddenly disappearing from their bank accounts—but it's going to a very good cause."

"I'd like to think they would see it that way, but frankly, they don't care much about anyone other than themselves. It's only their own futures they want to protect, along with their investments."

Walter looked confused. "Jason, why are *you* doing this? It's your uncle's vision that you're seeking to derail."

Jason appeared distracted. "I'm questioning my role in facilitating that vision. I'm seeing things somewhat differently now."

Jake chimed in. "Wait a minute. It's hard for me to believe we can simply take 15 trillion dollars out of bunch of bank accounts, just like that, and not trigger a whole host of consequences. And how will it work?"

"There's risk, of course," said Snapdragon. "But I've done this before. Money in bank accounts is really nothing more than digital numbers in a computer. I'll insert a kind of smart virus that will cause the accounts to dump a preset amount of money into an intermediary cloud account that I'll set up. That account will then be directed to transfer the funds to the destination accounts that Walter will designate. As soon as the funds leave the cloud, the cloud account will self-destruct, leaving no trace of its existence."

"What about the firewall and security protocols? How do you get around them?"

"I have some procedures that allow me to do an end run around an opposing team before they know what's happening. I'll leave it at that. The trick is to build the right kind of virus for the situation. Once in, the virus tells the home account that nothing has changed, no money has been removed. It creates a dummy numeric placeholder for the amount that's been debited from the account. Eventually, they'll discover the balances in their accounts are different from what they expect, but by that time the money will have been distributed."

Then Snapdragon added, "And they can't really make a public fuss about it because the money is not supposed to exist anyway."

The room remained silent as the team tried to imagine the reality of transferring $15 trillion in digital form and converting it into $15 trillion of actual, usable currency. It was mind-boggling.

Ariel broke the silence. "I need to change the subject. I'm sensing we're going to have company. When? I'm not sure, but I'm sweating a lot, so this is not a good sign."

"What else can you tell us," asked Jake, an edge to his voice.

"They know we're here."

"Who knows we're here?"

"I think Garrett Henry knows Jason's here at least. I don't know if he knows I'm here."

"How can you tell?"

"Well, I can't absolutely say. I just have a feeling that he knows."

"Jason," said Jake, impulsively, "do you have something to do with this?"

Jason was defensive. "Are you calling me a spy?"

Ariel intervened. "No way, Jake. I can vouch for Jason. He's no spy."

"Well, then, how else can this Henry guy know you're here?"

"Bugs and tracking devices are so small," said Snapdragon. "They can be placed almost anywhere, on anything. Jason or even Ariel might be carrying one and not be aware of it. I suggest we start here—in this room. I have something that might help. Let's take a ten minute break."

The room was thick with tension. Cordiality and trust gave way to an atmosphere of intense suspicion. The ten-minute wait seemed interminable.

Snapdragon returned with a small electronic device. She stepped over to Ariel and scanned her from head to toe. Without comment, Snapdragon walked over to Jason and did the same. Still no results. She seemed confused.

"The briefcase," noted Jake. "Jason had a briefcase with him when he arrived on the ship. Test that."

Jason reached behind a nearby table and lifted up his briefcase and laid it on the table. Snapdragon scanned the case and her scanner responded with a sharp electronic tone. "Looks like we found our bug. Can you open the case for me?"

Jason entered a combination of numbers into the keypad and with a click the locks retracted. Snapdragon scanned the top and inside of the case. The scanner's tone reached its highest pitch on the right side corner of the case. She examined it closely and discovered a seam that looked out of place. She removed a pen-knife from her pocket, cut into the case and removed a slim silver metallic and plastic object slightly larger than a watch battery. She turned around and held it up for the group to view.

All eyes turned toward Jason. "Looks like you have some explaining to do," said Jake.

Jason waved his hand over the case. "This was my father's brief-case. I take it with me everywhere I go, but I have no knowledge of the tracking device. You'll just have to believe me."

"Then how did it get there?" asked Jake, his voice thick with obvious distrust of Jason's comment.

"I have no idea. I always keep it close to me. It's the only direct, physical connection I have with my father. He died when I was young."

Ariel came to Jason's defense. "Anyone could have tampered with it. How about your uncle?"

"Well, he did give it to me after my father died. It was recovered from the crash debris."

"And he could have placed the tracker in it then. Right?"

Jason pondered Ariel's hypothesis. "Now that you mention it, he always seems to know where I am."

"Including now," said Ariel.

"Including now," agreed Jason.

The discussion seemed at an impasse. Snapdragon spoke up. "Okay. So we're targeted. It's never good to have a bulls-eye on your back. We need to remove ourselves from the zone of fire."

"So what do you suggest?" asked Jake.

"If Jason is on the level, I challenge him to follow through on the money transfer."

"I'm ready. The account numbers are in the briefcase in digital form."

"Walter," said Snapdragon, "you said you could establish a secure high-speed wireless link with your shore facilities. Can you set us up with that now?"

"Certainly can," said Water. "I'll have it ready in fifteen minutes."

"Sooner is better."

"Can we believe Jason?" Jake asked the group. "Who knows what kind of information is being transferred about us."

"I doubt if it can transmit audio," noted Snapdragon, examining the bug more closely. "It's simply transmitting a GPS signal, like your smartphone. Still, that places us at risk. If we're going to do this money transfer thing, we'd better do it soon. We don't know what might be coming at us."

"I can tell you something about that," offered Ariel. "It's coming by water and air."

A knock on the cabin door got Walter's attention. He opened it and the crewmember handed Walter a small piece of paper. Walter read it aloud to the rest of the group. "Radar is picking up surface vessels heading our way and a small aerial object as well."

"How much time do we have?" asked Jake.

"Hard to tell. Depends on how fast they're going. But considering the range, maybe forty-five minutes for the boats, but the aircraft could arrive much sooner."

"I'll have to work fast," said Snapdragon.

Walter took the initiative, "We'll use the bug as a decoy. We'll keep it here on *Opportunity* and try to outrun them. In the meantime, the rest of you will escape on the *Skysaber* to my estate."

Just as Walter finished his sentence, another crewmember entered the room. "Sir, we've picked up a drone we think is about thirty miles out. It's flying towards us."

"Well then, taking the launch to the *Skysaber* won't work," said Catherine. "That drone will have a camera on it. They'll see us leaving. What's our plan B?"

"Plan B," said Walter, "is you use the *Opportunity's* minisub to board the *Skysaber*. Jason, can your ship take in a sub?"

"Yes, if it's not too big. I can flood a compartment."

"Then you guys prepare to evacuate the *Opportunity* and make for the *Skysaber*. Take it underwater far enough away so you won't be noticed."

"What about you, the crew and the ship?" asked Catherine. "You'll be a sitting duck."

"We're clearly at a disadvantage and we don't carry guns. But the *Opportunity* can be very fast when she needs to. Don't worry about me. Just get those funds transferred and get the hell out of here."

CHAPTER TWENTY SEVEN

Snapdragon set up three laptop computers on a table in the Captain's cabin and was furiously keyboarding as various security screens appeared and disappeared on the middle laptop. Following twenty minutes of intense focus, her face finally relaxed. "We're in," she announced triumphantly to Jason who was sitting beside her. The other two screens came alive with long columns of bank account numbers. "That's them," he said, amazed.

"Well then, I'm ready for the transfer. Are you still okay with this?"

"Affirmative."

"Here goes $15 trillion into the cloud . . . Poof!"

Snapdragon keyed in several more instructions. The screen displayed a barrage of transactions. "And off that goes to Walter's 1,000 accounts . . . and now the cloud account never existed."

"Pretty slick," admitted Jason. "You're good."

"Thanks," said Snapdragon with a confident smile. "But no one likes to lose trillions of dollars. We can expect pushback."

Walter entered the room. "It's done," Snapdragon said, leaning back in her chair and placing her hands behind her head. "The money is in the accounts."

"Fantastic. So much suffering will be relieved; so much good can come of it. But you both need to leave *now*. A small armada of attack crafts is approaching us."

Jason and Snapdragon packed up the computers into several briefcases. Assisted by two crewmembers, they hustled out the door and rushed to the ship's elevator to join with Catherine, Ariel, Razr and Jake.

As the team was preparing to evacuate the ship, the *Opportunity* was readying itself for survival. Harrison would remain behind to make sure he could get every ounce of power out of its Universal Energy drive engines, as the ship and its crew's safety now depended on outrunning its pursuers.

Walter took his place in cockpit along with his First Mate and Harrison. He issued his instructions: "Furl sails, extend rails, lower masts and prime the engines."

The words were barely out of Walter's mouth when a large explosion split the center mast in two. Pieces of sail, communication equipment, plastic and metal came showering down on the deck. A second explosion caused a portion of the deck housing to burst into flames. Just as the evacuating team was crossing the deck to the elevator that would take them to the minisub, both Jake and Ariel were thrown hard against the side of the elevator entrance housing and knocked unconscious. Jason, Razr and Snapdragon pulled Ariel and Jake inside, and for the moment ignored the blood that was now staining their clothes. Catherine closed the elevator doors, making sure everyone was protected, her ears still ringing from the sounds of the explosions and falling debris clattering across the ship's deck.

The *Opportunity* vibrated as the hydraulics pulled the remaining sails into their protective containers. The remaining two masts telescoped into the hull. Outside the hull, two long rails emerged from below the waterline and running the length of the ship. As soon as the "Rails Fully Deployed" text message appeared on the dashboard in the cockpit, Harrison activated the water jets and fired up the twin 9,000 horsepower generators.

Walter watched his control console anxiously, waiting for the indication that the team had safely launched the minisub. He knew the *Opportunity* could not withstand more direct hits and remain afloat. She had to begin running fast or perish in a mass of explosions.

Catherine and Snapdragon grasped Ariel's limp body, and Jason and Razr struggled to drag Jake along the corridor that led to the minisub. The crewmember assigned to help them escape ran ahead to open the doors to the watertight bunker and fire up the sub's power systems. The team stumbled inside the small underwater craft. There was just enough room for six people and the pilot. Snapdragon closed the doors behind them and turned the locks. Immediately, the sub's pilot remotely opened the hull door and water began flooding into the ship's launch compartment. Inside the sub, the occupants could feel the dull bursts of explosive impacts on the *Opportunity's* deck and hull. With a rush of compressed air, the minisub broke free of the ship. Jason joined the sub's pilot and directed him to take the sub alongside the *Skysaber*, still resting quietly submerged several hundred yards away. With the *Skysaber's* remote control he opened an underwater airlock to receive the sub into its interior compartment.

Back in the pilothouse of the *Opportunity*, Walter had received the electronic signal he was waiting for. "Power up now!" he shouted to Harrison. "Get us out of here. See those two ships coming towards us? We'll surprise 'em by rushing right between them. It'll take them time to turn around, but by then we'll be gone."

Harrison eased the twin lever controls forward as thousands of kilowatts rushed into the electric motors powering the twin water jets. The *Opportunity* rose up above the water onto its twin rails as the oncoming crafts attempted to surround it and close in for the kill. Much to the surprise of its attackers who considered the ship trapped, the *Opportunity* quickly accelerated to 45 knots (50 mph) and raced toward the incoming crafts, passing them in a blur. The *Opportunity* had temporarily escaped its circle of death.

The pilots of the attacking boats, dumfounded by their quarry's unanticipated maneuver, reacted by attempting to pivot their crafts 180 degrees, creating chaos in the water. Harrison now had the *Opportunity* at full throttle, high on its rails and skimming speedily across the water's surface. The ship, though, had suffered serious damage, was rapidly taking on water, and several crewmembers were critically injured. Harrison knew they'd not make it back to port if they sustained any additional damage. Walter, too, was aware of their potentially fatal situation and was attempting to call the Coast Guard for assistance, but most of their communication equipment had been destroyed.

Aboard the *Skysaber*, Ariel was rapidly losing blood. Her healthy green color had changed to an ashen grey. Catherine, Razr and Snapdragon were focused on doing what they could to administer to Ariel and Jake. As the aircraft finally achieved sufficient distance from the attack zone to avoid detection, it exited the water and made for Walter's estate. Its passengers, meanwhile, were doing their best to suppress their worst case fears of losing two beloved family members and dear friends.

CHAPTER TWENTY EIGHT

"It looks like a war zone down there," Razr muttered as Jason piloted the *Skysaber* over Walter's fire-ravaged estate. Gone was its harmonious symmetry, broken by the collapse of several key walls. The adjacent gardens and lovingly-tended grounds were corrupted with piles of blackened debris.

As the ship landed on the wide cobblestone driveway in front of the main entrance, Jason, Razr, Snapdragon and Catherine immediately moved Ariel and Jake into the still-intact entrance hall. Razr set off to find a suitable room to convert into a temporary medical clinic. Jason and Catherine carefully placed Jake and Ariel into beds. Snapdragon had done her best to stop the substantial loss of blood that both Ariel and Jake had suffered. The impact of the explosions had thrust both of them against hard, sharp surfaces and both had numerous bruises on their bodies. No bones, however, seemed broken.

"Why not take them to a hospital?" asked Jason. "I saw some vehicles on the premises when we flew over the property."

"We need to wait," Snapdragon cautioned. "We don't know whether it's safe to expose ourselves in public just yet. We *are* being hunted—and that was before we transferred the money. Now we've really stirred up the hornet's nest. Let's keep our heads down as long as we can."

"Jake's coming around," said Catherine as she bathed his forehead with the cool, wet towel she managed to prepare in a nearby bathroom that still had running water. "But I don't see any signs of consciousness in Ariel."

"Her breathing seems fine but very faint," said Snapdragon. "I'm going to look for some local herbs that might help her. It seems she's in a coma."

"I'm really concerned about her color, I've never seen her look so pale. It's like her life-force is draining away."

Razr was sitting across the bed from Catherine. He was staring intently at Ariel's face. "You know what I think? I think she's suffering not just from physical trauma, but also from some kind of psychic attack. There's more going on here than just ordinary wounding."

"That's not what I want to hear," Catherine scolded.

"I suggest we let her be for now, but we need to keep watch."

As evening approached, the intensity of the day had caught up with everyone. They were exhausted. One by one, they fell asleep in overstuffed chairs and sofas.

While still appearing unconscious to those ministering to her comatose body, Ariel's mind was working overtime. She imagined she was traveling through the skies with Jason in the *Skysaber*. They passed over the boreal forests of northern Canada, barely visible in the early dawn light. The huge watery expanse of Hudson Bay slid beneath them, glowing sunrise colors brightening the dark liquid. She watched with fascination as they reached the open waters of the southern Arctic Sea, now almost devoid of ice. Dead ahead, the great white island of Greenland emerged out of the mist.

"There. Down there," Ariel said, pointing toward the steep, white edge of the southwestern coast. Jason slowed the craft to a nominal 30 mph. Ariel narrated: "Greenland holds the world's largest ice sheet. It's melting fast, much faster than the scientists predicted. It's the Jackobshavn Glacier we want to see. Bring the ship down to the water level, right in front of the glacier and let's take a look."

As the craft settled 200 feet above the water, Jason carefully positioned the ship a good distance away from the flotilla of icebergs that populated the water. They watched the towering edges of the massive glacier shudder, shatter and collapse into the icy waters. Tons of vertical ice and snow crumbled before their eyes as if succumbing to a controlled demolition. "This glacier is melting into the ocean at the rate of about two football fields a day. Very bad. It's the snow and ice that reflect heat back into the atmosphere. If, or rather, *when* all the ice in Greenland melts, it would raise sea levels about seven meters or twenty-five feet, dooming many coastal cities, ocean islands, and millions of square miles of farmlands. Coastal cities would be largely uninhabitable in forty or fifty years. The loss of the ice all over the globe is *already* radically changing the climate of the whole planet."

In silence they continued to observe ragged, black-speckled white monoliths the size of the Empire State Building slip ingloriously into the sea. Ariel found herself dodging waves of grief that threatened to overtake her. She tried to vocalize her feelings: "It's like I'm watching some great, wise being slowly dying. That ice is an archive holding hundreds of thousands of years of Earth's history—its ancient memory. And now it's gone, dissolved into the ocean. Lost forever."

CHAPTER TWENTY NINE

Slumped against Ariel's still unresponsive body, Catherine awoke startled and shivering. She sensed there was something she needed to do, but she had difficulty defining just what it was. Hearing the sound of someone approaching, she rose and walked toward the door. It was Razr.

"You got the message, too? I have a strong feeling that we need to use the healing power of the lake to help Ariel. There's something there for us."

As they walked down the pathway to the shore of Lake Michigan, Catherine felt a tractor beam of energy drawing her toward the water. Wrapping her scarf around her neck, she stepped onto the dock that thrust 120 feet into the still lake. A vanilla moon hung suspended in the obsidian sky.

At the end of the wooden dock, Catherine stooped down, reached into the water, and cupped her hands together. She lifted the water, holding it reverently as it slipped through her fingers. She spoke to it: "Help . . . We need help with healing." Catherine projected her thoughts into the water. Razr offered a song in his native dialect—a special prayer to the spirits of water. Following Catherine's plea and Razr's incantation, a swirl of silver mist began to rise from the lake barely fifty feet from where they stood. It spiraled round and round, moving closer to them as if pushed by an unseen hand.

Catherine blinked: vision or reality? As the mist drew closer, it ascended into the air—two feet, four feet, six feet, eight feet. It grew denser, the moonlight offering enough illumination to give form to a shape: a gossamer woman in a flowing blue robe, her face suffused with energy, a crystal cup of water in her hand. The shadowy form moved toward Catherine, gliding effortlessly across the water's surface. Catherine felt her heart opening up wider than she ever dreamed possible. And from the ethereal lady's lips came a gentle yet firm voice, "Water is a living being, embracing the world, gifting the world with life. Water can heal when treated with respect and gratitude—if not, it will sicken and kill. Water is the mirror of the human condition, the human soul. Take this sacred water and heal." The mysterious woman then offered the glowing cup of water to Catherine, who gratefully received it.

No words other than those of the spirit woman were spoken in the still night air. Catherine thanked the generous lady silently: *It will be put to good use. I will carry your message to those willing to listen.*

The spirit woman dissolved into the darkness. Catherine and Razr hurried back to the estate. Catherine lovingly spread the precious liquid on Ariel's body, dabbing the water on her lips, forehead, heart, hands and feet, accompanied by loving words and thoughts.

At dawn, no immediate change was apparent in Ariel's condition. Catherine and Razr continued to sit with her, each holding one of her hands, sending healing energy. But by midday, Ariel's pulse strengthened, her body began to revive and her skin glowed. Everyone was encouraged by the changes. "Ariel is coming back," Catherine announced joyfully.

Ariel's recovery, though, was complicated by her near-constant dreams and visions: glaciers melting, plastics clogging the oceans, chemicals and effluents pouring into rivers and streams, toxic hydrocarbons pumped into the earth, underground aquifers vacuumed dry by thirsty irrigation systems, and pharmaceuticals contaminating lakes and groundwater. The images were profoundly depressing and overwhelming. Ariel remained exhausted.

"How about that small cottage?" suggested Jake. "It's quiet there and the porch overlooks the water. I think it will be good for Ariel to have some private time with the lake."

Catherine and Razr both agreed. Razr offered to help Ariel get settled in. Jason, respectfully witnessing the close bond between Catherine, Ariel, Jake and Razr, decided to remain silent.

Ariel found the cottage a safe place to find refuge from the autumn chill and her troubling visions. Sensing that the visions were a strong call for help, she pondered how to respond. Settling into a comfortable chair in front of the fireplace, the mesmerizing golden light enfolded her. Ariel slipped into a trance. Time and space shifted. Now unmoored from her normal, conscious state, Ariel began to notice images appearing between the flames—shadows and faint tree-shaped forms. A large bird emerged from behind the trees, gliding right and then left. It called out in a guttural voice as it flew again across the scene and was gone. Flocks of birds followed it, flying erratically, struggling to stay airborne, some dropping suddenly out of the sky. A long line of animals marched single-file through desiccated forests, across dreary plains and sun-bleached deserts, staggering and collapsing, their bodies instantly vaporizing as they fell to the ground.

A log crackled in a burst of sound. Ariel's trance deepened and she mentally attempted to envision herself as a comforting lighthouse, generating a beacon of welcome illumination, with a promise of safe harbor to the weary and exhausted creatures in her harrowing dream. And then it appeared: a speck of movement in the midst of the chaos of writhing life-forms. It traveled across the landscape, glided towards her and settled to the ground. The feathered creature retracted its wings and stood still in front of her. Ariel stretched out her blanket, spreading it as wide as her arms could go—and the bird leapt forward into the blanket's embrace, wild bird becoming man. She knew it was Razr, returning from one of his shapeshifting missions with the animals. And she also knew he would be called back often by the many endangered species, now teetering on the brink of extinction. A disturbing awareness gripped her: so many, so fast now. They are the walking dead.

Razr had been sitting on the outside porch imagining himself in the woods meeting with his animal allies. He felt an urgency and rushed into the living room, sensing that Ariel needed help. He put his hands on Ariel's heart, singing an ancient song that he had learned during his youth in the jungle. Razr understood how the power of song could assist people to relax when in a stressful situation.

As Ariel found her way back to conscious awareness, she and Razr sat face-to-face and heart-to-heart, in full communion. Without needing words, they both felt the world pulling them to ever-more challenging tasks, but this moment was theirs: to celebrate their love.

"Ariel, I'm here for you."

Ariel soaked in the raw energy of desire fixed in Razr's voice. Razr reached forward to this luxuriant woman who openly awaited him. He touched her face, running his hand softly against her cheek and lovingly through her auburn hair now glowing, backlit by the dancing firelight. He drew her to him and their lips met. They were both surprised how quickly the personal stories and life-spaces between them vanished. Feeling the need to merge warm flesh and heart together, they welcomed the opportunity to explore each other's nakedness with eyes and hands. Soon, the fire's illumination was outlining the shadows and secrets of their pleasure. They lost themselves in each other, slipping into the realm of infinite possibilities, hearts beating in close synchrony. The sounds of love mingled joyously with the combustive exhilaration of primal fire. Outside, a soft-focus moon stood guard in sacred silence.

CHAPTER THIRTY

The next morning

Ariel was not sure whether or how to bring up the subject with Razr. She fiercely resisted any thoughts that would detract from the blissful night they had shared together. But she had questions . . .

"Just before you came into the room last night . . . It was about the animals. I'm afraid for them."

Razr was startled, but not surprised.

"The earth knows; the animals know," he said with uncharacteristic seriousness. "They can feel what's happening to them."

"And?"

"They feel the loss. When one species goes, the whole multi-million year history of its relationship to other species in its eco-relationship dies with it. A hole is created in the body of existence—'a disturbance in the Force,' you might say. It may seem inconsequential to those who have become so detached from the natural world, but it *is* felt by those to whom this world is their universe."

Ariel was now fully joined with Razr in his awareness. "I see what we're losing. It's something I feel, too."

Razr frowned. "People tell us how animals can do such amazing things—like predicting the weather, traveling long distances without maps and GPS equipment, showing us how to die gracefully as they provide us with food. And consider how some plants can cure fevers and cancers."

"So, what's wrong with that?"

"Nothing. It's just that we always talk about what we can *take* from nature; how we can *commodify* nature. We don't think about what we can *give* to nature. That's what I'm talking about. *Reciprocity.* Nature needs *us* to step up to the plate . . . like right now.

"The problem is—we fail to ask the question: Where do our resources come from—the metal, the plastic, and the electricity that brings artificial life to our technologies? We also fail to remember that just beyond the edge of our awareness exists a whole more-than-human world waiting—waiting to be acknowledged; to be respected; to be appreciated; to be listened to; to be protected and to be *healed* when necessary. And inside that rich and sensual world lives a natural intelligence that is deeply infused with ancient archives of knowledge and wisdom that we ignore at our peril."

"And the whole world is in peril," said Ariel, moving herself close to Razr. She grasped his hands in hers and their eyes connected. "I understand what you're saying. I sense these losses every day as a photosynthesizer."

Ariel paused, suddenly realizing where she was headed. Should she stop right here? She yearned to ask Razr again if he would consider joining her. But would he say "no," like last time in the Nevada desert . . . and leave? She decided not to chance it.

"What? What were you about to say?" he asked, suspecting she had stumbled across something unspeakable.

Ariel changed her mind and decided to go for it. "It was about asking you something that's so important to me—to join me—by modifying your genetics. You and me, together, as photosynthesizers."

Razr leaned back in his chair, stretching his feet out straight. He raised one hand to his jaw and slowly rubbed it in thought. Ariel scrutinized his face, hoping for agreement, but fearing rejection. She waited.

"I'm already not totally human," he said, his face exhibiting an ancient knowing far beyond his years.

"Of course. I understand that. I mean . . . how can you change from animal to human? Where does that really come from?"

"It's old, very old, from the earliest time—when people and animals lived together. Then a person could become an animal and an animal could become a person. Sometimes a person, sometimes an animal, and they all spoke the same language."

"So, how about this: What if it were possible to merge your abilities and shapeshifting skills with the light-energy and transformative nature of photosynthesis? Imagine the possibilities that could result." Ariel faced Razr and asked with love, "Will you join me and help create Human 3.0?"

CHAPTER THIRTY ONE

Lake Albion Valley

Garrett Henry was furious.

He had hurriedly summoned his legion of financial co-conspirators. They needed to craft a response to what he considered a most appalling breach of their formerly impregnable fiscal fortress.

These self-described Masters of the Universe and Holders of All the Cards controlled an almost unbelievable $50 trillion in financial assets with which to restructure the world to their design and benefit. Yet they considered the surprise debit to their off-balance-sheet accounts an "egregious thievery of the highest order."

Once the fleet of private jets had been securely parked on the valley runway, his guests prepared themselves for what they expected would be a rather tumultuous meeting. The elite group filed into the grand conference room. And Garrett Henry did not disappoint. "We've been royally hacked," he said, his voice bellowing. "Several days ago, someone broke through our security system. They figured out our codes and defeated our encryption protocols. I thought we had the best of the best working for us, but somehow the thieves got through."

"How bad is the damage?" asked a man from Belgium.

"I'm told about $15 trillion is missing," said Garrett, fuming.

"What's the remaining balance?"

"If we deduct about $18 trillion in stranded fossil assets—about $17 trillion."

Most of the group's heads nodded in relief.

"It could have been worse," commented the man from Belgium. "Seventeen trillion is enough to work with."

Garrett snarled. "Fifteen trillion dollars! In the wrong hands, that amount of money can cause a lot of damage to our program goals."

"Can you be more specific?" asked a woman from Brazil.

"I will remind you that our plan is to privatize the majority of global freshwater sources and associated distribution infrastructure. We already own three of the five major international water treatment and provider corporations and are working to buy majority interest in the others. We know that water has far more value as an economic good than as a human right, and we focus on urban areas because that's where the money is. Poor people don't pay. We say to them 'no money, no water.'"

"But can we simply ignore all those who can't pay?" asked the woman, expressing concern.

"Our PR line is: 'We'll get to them later.' We tell the press 'we're working for the planet.' That usually gets them off our back for a while. But let's not forget that providing good water to the two billion plus people that have no access to it will simply allow too many people to live, and healthy poor people provide no economic return. They are of no value to us."

Garrett Henry noted no immediate response to his last statement. He was greeted with blank stares indicating that no one dared challenge Henry's sociopathic plans.

"But back to the issue at hand: We need to address this very serious situation. It demands action."

"Any idea how this happened?" asked a man with a crisp British accent.

"We suspect the attack originated with the troublesome do-gooders in the Midwest. I've already ordered our agents in the area to do as much physical and psychological damage to them as possible."

"But how did—?"

"I'm convinced that Walter Langenstein and his team of misfits acquired our account numbers and passwords. That still wouldn't have been enough to disable our security system, but some very clever people tricked our servers into thinking nothing had changed, when in fact a massive withdrawal from multiple accounts had occurred. We discovered all this much too late. The money was then long gone."

"Can't we recover it?" exclaimed the woman from Brazil. "It's our money."

"We elected to keep this money outside the global financial accounting system. Our latest audit shows we had $20 trillion in offshore accounts and another $25 trillion in unregistered and undeclared accounts in banks and various other secure locations. We don't want the regulators or the taxing authorities to know this money exists."

Garrett paced back and forth across the room staring at the carpet, thinking.

He stopped and addressed the group. "And it gets worse: The New York ARCbank has reported a significant amount of gold was shipped to an undisclosed location. I'm still working on tracking that down. However, there *are* things we can do to move things along toward our important goals and stymie the efforts of those who would love to thwart our progress."

"Such as . . ." asked the man from Belgium.

Garrett was now hitting his stride. "Several days ago I ordered an attack on a ship in Lake Michigan that Langenstein uses as a sort of floating headquarters. The ship was seriously damaged and may sink before it reaches port. I've instructed our agents in Africa, South America and Asia to obstruct, confound and destroy the projects Langenstein and his Climate Justice Center or whatever it's called will try to roll out. That's our top priority. I've also ordered our teams to infiltrate their administrative operations, sabotage their materials and contaminate their sites and supplies in the U.S. and elsewhere. And I've instructed our financial teams to accelerate our water privatization efforts. This will make it more difficult for them to acquire access to so-called common areas of agricultural land and water sources. That should slow them down."

"Excuse me, Garrett," said the man from Belgium, "You said someone provided the account information. Do you know who that 'someone' might be? It had to be a party with inside knowledge of our financial records."

Garrett turned self-consciously toward the large windows that looked to the mountains and the valley below. The group awaited his response. It was hard, very hard for him to respond. Reluctantly, he turned and faced the group, his voice uncharacteristically weak. "I'm sorry to say that the intelligence I've received indicates that it was my nephew, Jason, who provided the critical information."

CHAPTER THIRTY TWO

The Cottage

Razr's strained face told the story. "I can't Ariel. I just can't."

Ariel looked away, disappointed.

"It's not about you," Razr insisted. "My feelings for you are strong and deep. It's about my . . . I guess, my mission . . . my purpose in life. And I'm afraid."

"Why afraid?" Ariel asked, as she pushed back against the tears building in her eyes.

"Afraid for the animals, the plants and the spirit beings. You see—I see myself as their translator, their representative in the human world. Like I said—the animals, the plants—they know what's happening. They try to be patient. They see the fabric of the natural world unraveling, and they're powerless to do anything about it. They grieve in silence. Most humans have no idea this is going on. They're clueless. Because I can enter into that other world . . . be one of them, feel with them and communicate with them, I'm a bridge between the more-than-human world and the human world. If I can't do this, then who speaks for them?"

"But why *wouldn't* you continue to speak for them? I don't understand."

"I believe my genetic makeup is already somewhat different from a normal human. Otherwise I couldn't shapeshift. The photosynthesis conversion is pretty radical. I'm concerned that if I modify it further, I'd lose my ability to transform. This would be a tragedy I'd never recover from."

Razr stood up and paced back and forth. "When I take on the shape and spirit of Panther, Coyote or Raptor, I'm also downloaded with their evolutionary history. It's so overwhelming and at the same time, *simple*. Sure, it seems like their lives are hard compared to ours, but there's a kind of acceptance of life and death because they, much more than humans, are able to be truly in the present and seem to deeply understand their place in the larger, universal scheme of things. They feel in ways we can't comprehend. They ask me: What's wrong with the humans? Why don't they care? How can they do this to us when we've been so good to them? We've done so much for them. Just consider the incredible contribution horses have made to human development . . . I'm sorry; I can't take any chances that might cut me off from them. I just can't do it . . . not even for you."

Ariel was taken aback by Razr's emotional outpouring. At first, she felt pushed away, like she belonged to some other world. Yet at the same time, she just flat-out loved his passion, his empathy, his caring for the universe of what he called 'more-than-human' species, and she certainly understood the need to protect them.

Her mind swirled as she tried to find a way around Razr's argument. "Aren't there other shapeshifters who can do this?"

"Maybe. But I don't know any, and if there were, would they be willing to work with the human world? Be part of something like the ACJC where action can be taken to address the planet's most critical issues?"

"So you're the sole shapeshifting spokesperson, for now, I guess . . ." Ariel's voice trailed off.

Razr grasped her hands in his. "Look, my decision about this in no way lessens the love I feel for you. I feel torn between my responsibility to the animal, plant and spirit world and my desire to create a future with you. I know there are great things we can do together . . . if we combine our skills and talents. It could be really amazing. It's already been amazing, but I have to remain true to my mission, my destiny. I don't know how I brought this on. Did I choose it? Or was it chosen for me? I don't know. But I do know I must follow it—wherever it takes me . . . and I want you to be part of it."

Ariel's psychic mind began flooding her with visions so strange she didn't even attempt to make sense of them. She struggled to balance the mental images in her head with a gnawing, sinking feeling in her heart. Getting control of herself, she finally responded. "I understand. I'm connected to the more-than-human world also—but in a different way. I'm not convinced adding the photosynthesis genes would disrupt your shapeshifting abilities in any way; but of course, I can't say that for sure. Maybe someday we'll know. So, in the meantime, yes—we can work together and certainly love together as well. I know that's possible and it's real . . . and it's right now."

Spontaneously, Ariel and Razr stood up together and embraced. Each held the other tightly, as if their love, their passion, and their commitment to people, animals, plants, and water were the only things preventing the world from imminent disintegration.

CHAPTER THIRTY THREE

City of Milwaukee
The American Climate Justice Collaborative

As the buzz of conversation in the conference room settled down, Walter spoke with undisguised excitement. "It's true. A significant amount of money has been received, and it will immediately be directed toward addressing urgent global programs. It's money that should have been made available decades ago for this purpose."

"How much money are we talking about?" asked Maria Campos, the ACJC Assistant Director.

Walter hesitated, anticipating the expected response. He lowered his voice. "Fifteen trillion dollars."

Mouths dropped open, and an audible gasp filled the room.

"I know that's an unbelievable amount of money, and I want to put it to work ASAP."

Contagious enthusiasm rippled across the room.

"When do we start?" asked Maria.

"I'm just as anxious as you are to get going. We need to work fast because there's another factor at work here. I've just received reports from our reps in the field that water delivery trucks have been sabotaged, equipment has been stolen, and government officials are revoking our operating permits in many of our key operational zones."

"Is there a connection to the money we've just received?" Maria understood the implications.

"Ah, they're here!" Walter said, as he turned toward the seven men and women who had just entered the conference room. "Good to see you all again!" he called in their direction.

Walter shifted his attention back to the staff. "These folks are the real heroes. Someday you'll know the full story. The short version is: We were sailing aboard my ship *Opportunity* when we came under armed attack. We had to part ways under some difficult circumstances. The *Opportunity* just barely made it back to port. But now, everyone's here, and we're ready to kick some serious ass."

Walter continued, "To answer Maria's question: Yes, the two things *are* linked. To better explain the connection, I'll ask Jason to provide some background."

Jason stepped to the front of the room. "My name is Jason Henry and I can speak to what's happening. There are certain people in the world who have a very different agenda than yours. In fact, what they seek to accomplish is the direct opposite of your goals. Whereas you see water as a basic human right that should be made available to everyone, these people view water only as a valuable commodity to be sold to the highest bidder. They are fully aware that water is central to the economic well-being and survival of humanity. However, they do not consider the survival of humanity as a whole a positive outcome. And the fact remains: You are disrupting their game plan."

"So we push back," said Walter, "and we move forward with smart thinking and creative counter-measures. We overwhelm whatever opposition is marshaled against us through strategic deployment of our projects. And remember: We now have our own very considerable financial resources. We are a force to be reckoned with."

A murmur of approval emanated from the group.

"I propose we start by discussing how we can put the funds to work. I've asked the ACJC to host a teleconference to allow people in our networks to weigh in. To our audience we will pose the question: How can we use the money for best results? The teleconference is scheduled for tomorrow morning."

The next day

Walter hosted the teleconference for identification of high-priority funding categories. The recommendations were as follows:

- Phase out the use of fossil fuels for energy production

- Eliminate malnutrition

- Provide universal sanitation

- Provide debt relief to impoverished countries, small farmers and students

- Provide clean and sufficient water for all

- Develop universal healthcare with an emphasis on contraception and disease prevention

- Provide universal educational and training opportunities

- Aggressively promote plant-based diets

- Provide immediate assistance to climate, political and economic refugees

- Institute a global jobs program

- Rebuild critical infrastructure

- Promote Fair Trade economic relationships

- Protect and restore ecologically-sensitive areas

- Restore and revitalize oceans and fisheries

As the discussion continued, a detailed spreadsheet was compiled listing the amounts proposed for each category. (See Appendix A).

"This is a great start," Walter exclaimed on the video feed. "What an amazing wish list. My math shows the amounts that have been proposed would total nearly $9 trillion. As an aside, I will note that it has been claimed that the U.S. Federal Reserve Bank cannot account for $9 trillion in loans, and at least $8.5 trillion is missing from various U.S. government budget records. We'll demonstrate better accountability and use some of the remaining $6 trillion to set up a World Stewardship Bank. The bank will make grants and low-interest loans to countries and communities in need— and without austerity requirements. We could also use the funds to generate additional money for future programs. It's important to ensure that we can continue this work indefinitely."

The enthusiasm generated by the teleconference was over-whelming. A Japanese woman called in to express what many others were sensing, "For the first time," she said, her voice vibrating with visceral emotion, "I feel that a more sustainable world may really be possible. Now *real* remedies for the root causes of disease, injustice, violence, and desperation can be applied."

A doctor from Germany made a plea: "Our hyper-consumptive patterns are not sustainable. We need to share what's left. I propose we find a way to shift our definition of quality of life from individual consumption to personal and community wellbeing. I know it won't be easy, but we must find a way."

But overshadowing the group's enthusiasm was the disturbing recognition that certain physical-world absolute boundaries could not, *must not*, be transgressed if humanity was to survive. Everyone knew that the global mean temperature was continuing to rise—now at almost 3 degrees Celsius higher than pre-industrial times, and the planet's supplies of freshwater, minerals, arable land and humanly-habitable space were fast running out. Optimists still held out hope that enough people, nations, corporations, institutions and governments could be convinced to work together to pull civilization back from the brink before an overwhelming cascade of calamitous events would finally seal humanity's fate.

As the process of implementation began moving forward, ACJC offices and conference rooms came alive with extraordinary ideas and imaginative designs for addressing the most critical needs and situations. Now, great ideas need not die or become shelved simply because the organization lacked sufficient funds. Good projects and programs deemed urgent and vital could move ahead in an expedited fashion.

But one issue, in particular, always seemed to rise to the top of the discussion.

CHAPTER THIRTY FOUR

The privatization of water.

The staff at the ACJC decided to convene an international summit in an attempt to develop a consensus on how best to cope with this divisive issue.

"We've got to take this head on," said a woman dressed in a colorful sari. "I see it everywhere in my country—selfish people trying to make money off something no one can do without. Something that should be accessible to even the poorest of the poor. What is the answer? How can we stop the greed?"

"Water is so basic," said another. "Withholding water from those who have no money is in reality a death sentence."

The volume of voices began to build as the frustration in the room continued to increase.

Catherine stepped up to the front of the ACJC conference room. She was deeply concerned about the ongoing conflicts over droughts and limited water availability. Violent clashes were becoming endemic. Impoverished refugees in search of food and jobs continued to surge across borders, further destabilizing governmental relationships. And often the source of the refugee problem was a lack of water for growing food and for living. The situation threatened to ignite a global water war. Her confident presence seemed to calm the tension and frustration that charged the room.

"The water," she said. "Perhaps the water itself can help us."

Catherine now had the full attention of the room. "We all know that water is life. Other than air, it's the one thing that's shared by every life-form on the planet. And consider that our bodies are 70 percent water and our cells are about 90 percent water. Water is part of our identity as human beings."

Catherine paused to allow her audience to absorb her words. She was preparing to introduce an even more radical concept: "We live in a reciprocal relationship with water. If we respect water, water will keep us alive. If we abuse it, we become sick. That's a given. Our relationship with water can be viewed as a mirror of the human condition. Unfortunately, the image in the mirror is not pretty. I propose we change this."

"But how?" asked a man gesturing with his hands, his eyes wide with curiosity.

"What if we could use the huge body of freshwater that lies just a mile from where we sit today, as a liquid, global communication medium?"

Heads began spinning, processing Catherine's provocative words.

Everyone in the ACJC was familiar with the facts around water. They knew that less than 2.5 percent of the world's water is freshwater. Most of that is locked up in glaciers, leaving only 1.2 percent that is usable by humans; and most of that is buried underground. Of the small fraction of surface water that's left—the Great Lakes, the largest freshwater system on the Earth—holds an astounding 20 percent.

Like the great prairie of the American Heartland, whose rich, grass-covered ecosystem appeared to offer an agricultural bonanza, the Great Lakes' aquatic bounty was similarly viewed as an inexhaustible resource. And like the ill-fated prairie, where rich topsoil was turned to airborne dust in but a few years, careless men employing shortsighted and inappropriate practices devastated the once-vast fisheries of the Great Lakes. Sadly, many rivers, bays and streams have become toxic wastelands due to poorly-regulated industrial and agricultural pollution. Consequently, formerly pristine aquifers have become saturated with poisonous chemicals and dangerous bacterial compounds, and many wells are now considered unfit for human consumption.

Though today's Great Lakes are woefully lacking in their early bounty of trout, sturgeon, and perch, the five lakes still exist as a vast ocean of freshwater, large enough to satisfy the thirst of entire nations. Yet, unthinking people continue to use them, like many other great bodies of water, as something to waste and use as a sewer, hoarding and marketing the resource for profit and power.

"Could you explain how this might be possible?" asked a woman, staring at Catherine.

"It works like this," Catherine said, drawing on her considerable scientific knowledge, "Consider that you have several tuning forks of the same frequency; you strike one, the others resonate as well. The information—the energy of sound—is transferred from one fork to the other."

The room filled with conversational voices as the group processed her provocative statements. An enthusiastic woman stood up and turned to face the audience. "I'm a physicist and we're constantly discovering new relationships on the molecular and atomic levels, even over great distances. It's a phenomenon called 'non-locality.' Every point in space and time provides an entry point to every other point in space and time. You make a change in one location, and that change or particular input is instantly duplicated at a distant location. This happens at the sub-atomic level."

"Is this the idea that when a butterfly flaps its wings in China it triggers a hurricane in Florida?" asked another woman in the group.

"Something like that," responded the physicist. "I think this is what Catherine is suggesting—that we could use the connectivity and conductivity inherent in the molecules in Great Lakes water to communicate with the greater sum of water molecules existing on the planet . . . and in the human body, which is mostly water."

"Or," suggested a computer wizard from Montreal, "I can imagine water serving as a programmable storage medium—a global flash-drive . . . a flash-drive that can be reprogramed."

Many in the group nodded approvingly.

Catherine gathered her thoughts together. She knew she had plenty of sympathetic listeners, but what she was about to propose would likely prompt a high degree of skepticism. Still, she was determined to go forward. She took the leap.

"This is my idea: We issue an invitation for people to join in a 'water respect day.' I think *respect* is the key to a new relationship between humans and water. We encourage people to gather at accessible points along the shoreline of all five Great Lakes and offer thoughts of appreciation and respect to the water. Those who live near other sources of water around the world can do the same, adding their own creative ideas to the process."

Catherine paused, allowing her words to find their mark in the hearts of all in the room. Her group of friends looked toward her, astonished and proud. Following the pause, Catherine asked from the deepest place she could find inside herself, "I suggest we call it 'The Great Lakes Water Gathering.' Are you with me?"

The room erupted with cheers, and Catherine was greeted with a standing ovation.

CHAPTER THIRTY FIVE

The public announcement of this most ambitious undertaking took place at the Milwaukee Art Museum, in the soaring and spacious Quadracci Pavilion designed by Spanish architect Santiago Calatrava. Its streamlined, graceful architecture featured a *brise soleil*, a set of twin 217-foot (66 meter) white wings that opened during the day and folded over the tall, arched structure at night. To the observer, the building appeared poised to leap into the air. This particular venue was chosen, not just for the emotional uplift that visitors experienced, but also for the view that the multi-storied, transparent lobby afforded of Lake Michigan's dramatic expanse just beyond.

As a key spokesperson for the ambitious project, Catherine looked radiant as she spoke with passion and intensity from the stage in the light-filled pavilion. Beyond the hundreds of windows, the blue-green surface of Lake Michigan stretched far to the right and far to the left and straight on to the horizon. It appeared like an endless ocean.

Catherine's voice wrapped around the two hundred plus people clustered in the grand space, assisted by the powerful audio system. "We all know how critically important healthy water is to life on this planet. Without clean water, life suffers. Every minute a child dies from a water-related disease. Over two billion people lack access to clean water. Even here in the United States, our domestic waters are becoming increasing polluted with legacy chemicals, pharmaceuticals, agricultural runoff and toxic metals. What we put in our water we put in our bodies. We can . . . we must . . . do better by our water. I'm asking you to join me in this long-overdue and vitally necessary undertaking. It is my sincere belief that if enough people are willing to focus on imparting a positive intent into water, locally and globally, then maybe, just maybe, humanity's self-destructive course can be altered. This is our opportunity for give-back."

The invitation was sent throughout the Great Lakes Region by social media, radio, television, print and personal persuasion. Residents of the area were asked to travel to their nearest body of water on the designated day and create a celebration or ceremony of their own design. It was also made clear that anyone, anywhere, was invited to participate. People around the world were encouraged to choose a local river, lake or stream and connect with the gathering in the Great Lakes Region. And of course, the bays and oceans of the world would also be included, as they cover 71 percent of the planet's surface and contain 97 percent of the world's water. Interestingly, the proportion of water in our bodies is the same as that of Planet Earth. The purpose of this collective action, therefore, was nothing less than a rebooting of the global human consciousness.

Jake took charge of special transportation logistics. Charter boats were dispatched to support people who were willing to travel to the more remote areas. Local residents volunteered their pickup trucks and cars for ground transportation.

Snapdragon and Razr were placed in charge of security. Razr would disappear for days at a time meeting with his animal allies and asking them to exercise special attentiveness regarding any kind of suspicious activities that might occur in the forests surrounding the lakes.

Snapdragon had recruited her network of computer geeks to monitor Internet traffic, especially sites deemed suspect such as weapons and chemical vendors. Jason assumed the job of handling the financial aspects of the undertaking. He personally contributed a check for one million dollars.

The Native Americans of the northern reservations agreed to provide food and shelter for local water pilgrims. For them this was something amazing—that so many non-Indians were now showing respect for water, which the Native People had always considered sacred.

Wonderfully creative events were slated to be held along the Great Lakes shorelines in Milwaukee, Chicago, Buffalo, Toledo, Cleveland, Detroit, Traverse City, Thunder Bay, Toronto, Sault Ste. Marie, Green Bay, Erie and Duluth.

Everyone at the ACJC mobilized to help ensure that the Gathering ran smoothly. Camps were set up in park areas, close to public beaches. Frontage roads were filled with cars as people made their way to accessible shorelines.

Bright sunlight greeted the eager participants on the day of the Great Lakes Water Gathering. As the hour approached high noon, men, women and children took up positions along the shores of lakes, rivers and streams. Some had arrived the night before, had greeted the dawn and were now sitting quietly, already focused on connecting intimately with the water. Each person chose his or her special spot and faced the water.

At 12:00 noon, Central Time, the participants throughout the world joined together to honor Water, each in their own way. Some began to feel the tears well up as they felt the union of human hearts and minds with the precious life-giving substance.

On a quiet beach along the southern shore of Lake Superior, a Native American elder dressed in her traditional tribal dress was joined by other Indigenous people who had traveled from around the continent to support the ceremony. Since she had personally walked the shoreline of all five Great Lakes, she was given the privilege of leading the ritual. She shared her thoughts and prayers with the participants. With a strong voice she expressed her appreciation to them as they joined together in reverence for the Great Waters. She spoke about how women are the Water Keepers and that water is called "the First Medicine."

Following a series of prayers in her native language, the graceful, elderly woman explained that water is the life-blood of Mother Earth. "Water courses through the body of Mother Earth and maintains life. Water is not a thing, but a living entity, a spirit." She reminded everyone that our first environment is water; that we live in water as we grow inside the womb. And then we are born—out of the womb, through water. "It is from this understanding that we can know our kinship with water—that we and water are One."

Pausing again for long seconds, she continued, this time her voice carried a deep sense of concern. She asked that everyone work to protect the headwaters, springs and lakes and rivers and oceans. "We need to change our relationship with the natural world from one of exploitation to one that recognizes the sacredness of water and All Life. Our waters suffer greatly from our abuse. Today, I ask each of you, in your own way, to make a commitment to heal your relationship with water."

A deep silence followed her remarks. Barely audible at first, the healing sounds of drumming and singing began to fill the air, carrying the spiritual offering to the Great Lakes—and to all the waters of the world.

CHAPTER THIRTY SIX

Milwaukee
Inside the ACJC

People began to notice the changes. Several days after the water ceremonies, those familiar with Great Lakes water conditions observed subtle improvements in water quality. Water analysts measured a significant increase in dissolved oxygen levels and noted less invasive algae around the shorelines. Since affiliated water gatherings had been held on six continents and countless towns and communities, it appeared that the event had struck a resonant chord with hundreds of thousands, possibly millions of people throughout the world. Weeks later, it was reported that many cities had reported a decrease in crime. Hospitals in Africa and India registered fewer patients with water-borne diseases. Though anecdotal, many believed that these changes were attributable to the Great Lakes Water Gathering.

After a day of rest, the team: Catherine, Ariel, Jake, Harrison, Snapdragon, Razr, Jason and Walter regrouped to debrief. As they settled themselves into Walter's ACJC office, it was clear that Jason Henry did not share in their exuberance. Catherine was the first to notice his sullen appearance. "Jason, are you alright?"

The rest of the group quieted down and turned toward Jason. Slumped in his chair, he straightened up when he felt their attention focusing on him. "To be honest, no . . . Everything that's happened recently has caused me to undertake some serious personal reflection. Growing up, I enjoyed all the privileges that money could buy. It's a world 99.9 percent of the population can only imagine in their wildest dreams. I have to ask: Why me? A lucky throw of the dice, I guess, or some other reason I can't fathom. But I can ride out whatever tragic calamities might befall civilization. So many of the people I've met have no such option."

Receiving no response, Jason continued, "Hell, I've got my own UFO, and until recently, I've had access to a completely functional underground city with everything you'd need to survive a nuclear holocaust or an uninhabitable surface . . . *and* live a full life there for decades if necessary. Or I could opt for transportation to other planets if need be."

"Are you referring to the rumored colonies beyond Earth?" asked Jake.

"There's a lot that's been going on that's been kept out of the public eye."

"It makes perfect sense," said Harrison. "Where do we think the ET guys have been hanging out?"

"Personally, I'd have zero interest in emigrating to another planet," argued Catherine. "I don't think there'd be many job openings for people like me on the moon or Mars. Geologists maybe, but certainly not wildlife biologists. Plus, there's no way I'm going to abandon my bears, birds and bees here on Earth. No way."

"Those are pretty dry places," noted Jake, shaking his head in mock disbelief. "I'd never consider living someplace so devoid of surface water."

Jason was becoming frustrated. "You can think what you want, but let me just say that I've been privy to discussions about the Mars settlement program. It's something that's been underway for decades."

"How are they getting there?" asked Jake.

"I've heard that two means of transportation are available: tele-portation—which works almost instantly—and regular transport by spacecraft that takes about 35 days one way."

The room went silent.

"Here's what I'm trying to say: I'm conflicted. I am—or at least I was—a privileged member of a parallel world that exists right now, right here. Ariel's called it a breakaway civilization, a good descrip-tion I think, because it has indeed broken away and separated itself from most of humanity's basic concerns and worries. And it has its own short- and long-term agendas—which we've often discussed are not supportive of the programs and values that the ACJC and its network of partners holds as important."

"Well," said Harrison, leaning forward in his chair, both arms propped on his knees and looking across the room at Jason. "If what you're saying is true, it would explain why there's so little effort being made to seriously address climate change and global warming by those in power. They've already got tickets on the last train out of town. You're a really lucky dude. You can choose the world . . . or *whichever* world you want to live on. You've got a free pass."

Harrison inhaled and shook his head. "Let's just say we're all on a ship called the *Titanic 2*. The ship's just hit the big iceberg and it's starting to go down. The first class passengers have already left the ship quietly in secret lifeboats reserved just for them. The climate change deniers are busy drinking at the bar and filling up with food from the buffet as if everything is AOK. Meanwhile, the rest of the ship's passengers are wondering what the hell is happening. Some of the smart ones know what's going on and are trying to get the Captain and the crew to either save the ship or deploy the lifeboats in an efficient manner before it's too late. Will they succeed? We don't know. But the first classers are already halfway to New York . . . or maybe to Mars."

Turning toward Jason, Harrison asked, "So Jason—the ques-tion to you is: Given what you've experienced here during the

past few months, do you intend to leave on the secret lifeboats—
or not?"

As tension in the room escalated, all eyes were fixed on Jason,
awaiting his reply.

CHAPTER THIRTY SEVEN

Jason cleared his throat. "I'm going back to BC."

Ariel's jaw dropped. "I can't believe you'd risk it."

Jason was firm. "I have to. I'm sure my uncle knows I provided you with the account codes and that I'm participating in ACJC activities. And I'm sure he's not happy that I had 800 metric tons of gold bars shipped out of that bank vault in New York. Facing him is the right thing to do, and I consider myself responsible for the consequences of my actions."

Ariel was quick to respond. "I'm implicated, too. I'm an accessory to the crime."

"It's not a crime," retorted Walter. "That gold and that money belong to all the people on the planet. A lot of it represents the illegal plunder of war. The fact is: A criminal cabal has used this fortune to set itself up as a kind of New Royalty. They've fleeced others of their wealth and then concentrated it in the hands of an elite few. Let's call it what it truly is—*financial terrorism*. It was time somebody pushed back, and we did, thanks to you and Jason."

"And the genius of Snapdragon." Jason smiled. She beamed back.

Ariel looked around the room. She saw her team. All that they had been through in the Northwest, the Southwest and the Midwest flashed before her eyes—the fear, the violence, and the successes. Was it time to do it again?

"I haven't mentioned this yet," said Ariel, with a touch of trepidation in her voice, "but late last night, just as I was falling off to sleep, I picked up something from either Debbie Chen or maybe my ET-hybrid contact there. I believe the photosynthesizers in BC are planning a revolt and maybe the underground workers as well. Definitely, trouble is brewing. I think we *all* need to go back. We need to mount an intervention."

Jake spoke up with passion. "It's time to expose those secret underground cities with their high-speed railroads and captive workers. The world needs to know about the refuge enclaves and the breakaway culture. We need to blow their cover. They're using up valuable natural resources, and worst of all, refusing to take any responsibility for the mess they've helped to create on this planet. They need to answer for it."

"We'll go to British Columbia," Harrison suggested, "and sneak into the underground city. We disguise ourselves as workers and make like we're doing routine maintenance. Meanwhile, we'll be taking photographs and video. Then we release everything to the media."

Walter was quick to join in. "This could lead to a serious public discussion of the matter. It's unconscionable that this is being kept hidden!"

Catherine was caught off guard by the sudden turn of events, but realized there was no time for careful deliberation. "I'm in."

"Me too," echoed Snapdragon. "I can't bail on you now that things might get nasty . . . And I miss Debbie." Snapdragon turned her head away, her voice becoming uncharacteristically emotional. "She's more than a friend to me." Everyone understood the deeper meaning of Snapdragon's statement and her feelings for Debbie Chen.

"You people are amazing," marveled Walter, dropping his shoulders, clearly moved emotionally. "I'd love to join you—"

"You need to stay here and keep the ACJC humming," interrupted Jake. "With the increasing conflicts over water and the millions of climate refugees flooding into other countries, you need to make sure the ACJC and its network of collaborators keep sticking their fingers in the many holes in the dike."

Ariel turned to Jason. "It's a courageous thing you're doing and it has a lot of integrity. I applaud you for making this decision."

Jason smiled self-consciously as the group trained their attention on him. "Sure, my uncle is a formidable man, but I can be too when it's necessary. And now it's necessary."

CHAPTER THIRTY EIGHT

The sky was overcast as the sleek *Skysaber* lifted off from the estate's grounds. Walter waved as the dark triangle diminished into the distance like a receding train. Feeling deep misgivings about their dangerous quest, he wished he could provide them with some measure of security, but there was nothing more he could do. Their fate would be determined by many factors, some predictable, most not.

Inside the *Skysaber*, Jason asked Jake to serve as pilot—as he needed to focus on preparing his strategy for dealing with Garrett Henry. Jake was pleased to have the controls of the highly responsive craft in his hands once again. Snapdragon had taken over planning the mission. She briefed the team: "Step One is to land near the photosynthesizer's camp. We have a small RV on board that I've equipped with surveillance and monitoring equipment. We'll pretend we're ordinary tourists checking out the valley's wineries. I'll be able to eavesdrop on communication traffic around the area and intercept the data streams between the various servers or shut them down, if necessary. We'll see what's needed once we get there. Catherine, Ariel, Razr and I will attempt to help with the photosynthesizer's insurrection at the compound, if that's really what it is. Step Two: Jake and Harrison will accompany Jason into the underground area and photo-document the place for later exposure to the public."

"What if Jake and Harrison are discovered?" asked Catherine. "What defenses do they have?"

Jason was quick to respond, "I've provided them with a schematic of the interior of the city, so they'll know their way around, and I've got standard worker uniforms aboard the *Skysaber* so they'll be well disguised."

"And how do we make our exit, assuming everything goes as planned?" asked Catherine.

"Jake and Harrison will use the Skysaber to pick the rest of us up," said Snapdragon, trying to sound confident, but realizing that many things could happen to disrupt their plans.

Catherine busied herself by scanning the Internet from the communications subunit on the bridge. A major news report caught her attention: A CBC camera crew had just returned from Eastern Siberia where an enormous volume of methane was discovered venting from the seabed and the permafrost. Scientists had been concerned that a methane burp could release the equivalent of thousands of tons of CO_2 into the atmosphere. A sudden charge of greenhouse gas such as this could overwhelm the northern climate system, triggering violent weather around the globe. Catherine decided to postpone mentioning this to the team, as they had other more immediate issues to deal with.

At Mach 3, the *Skysaber* arrived over British Columbia in 70 minutes. As Jake slowed the craft, Harrison and Jason stepped in front of the viewing windows to observe the Canadian Rockies pass beneath them. They were now approaching the Lake Albion Valley. Jake had activated maximum cloaking throughout the trip to ensure the element of surprise. Jake landed the *Skysaber* in a field hidden by a long line of dense pine trees. He released the loading hatch and ramp. Snapdragon fired up the van—looking like a small RV— and drove the vehicle onto the ground outside the ship. Catherine, Snapdragon, Ariel and Razr climbed inside. The van jostled its way to the nearby road. Once on the pavement, they watched as the *Skysaber* was airborne once again and vanished across the treetops.

With Snapdragon at the wheel, Catherine set the onboard GPS system to their desired destination. She turned to Ariel. "What's going on at the compound?"

Ariel's eyes were shut in concentration. "Everything's pretty quiet right now. I sense some kind of secret meetings are underway. But looking ahead, I see violent activity. I see trucks and military-like men moving toward the area. We need to warn our people there somehow."

"They don't have any idea we're coming, do they?" asked Razr. "Give me something in writing and I'll deliver it by airmail to Debbie Chen. But first show me on a map where she's located."

Neither Catherine nor Ariel spoke, knowing that the risk level had just been ratcheted up by several notches, but they both agreed it was a good idea. Snapdragon drove the van into a cluster of trees behind a barn and parked. After studying a map showing the location of the target area, Razr exited the van and walked behind the trees. Three minutes later, a large brown and white raptor was gliding toward them. Catherine reached out her hand, holding a paper note. The bird snapped it up, and with startling ease was soon soaring above the treetops. The bird tipped its wings right and left, circled once and was gone.

Snapdragon activated her surveillance system and Catherine kept an eye out for unwanted visitors. So far, everything seemed normal. A moderate amount of traffic rumbled along the two-lane road two hundred yards away. Ariel focused on remotely viewing the inside of the nearby underground city.

"It appears the conversations at the mountain aren't quite normal," noted Snapdragon. "I'm picking up some kind of uneasiness. Seems they're warning security people to be on high alert."

"Yeah, I'm sensing that too," said Ariel, "like they know something's up."

"Hey," said Catherine, tilting her head skywards. "Look at that angry sky over there. I think we might be in for some heavy weather."

Ariel opened the door of the RV and stepped outside. "It's settled over the mountain . . . right where the underground city is located."

CHAPTER THIRTY NINE

Jake was uneasy flying the *Skysaber* toward what appeared to be a solid wall of stone and dwarf pine trees. "I hope there's some kind of magic door there," intoned Harrison, his voice rising. "Otherwise they'll have to scrape us off the side of that mountain."

Jason activated the entrance portal control, and the appearance of solid rock dissolved into a kaleidoscope of color, revealing a long, rectangular opening just as the *Skysaber* came within 100 yards of the mountain's face. Even more surprising to Jake and Harrison was the size of the interior cavity and the presence of a much larger flying craft parked inside. Jake recognized the huge circular ship as that which he had seen many months before in the Nevada desert that carried Ariel and the photosynthesizers to points unknown.

"That's the ARV-3200xi," noted Jason. "It's the craft that's used to transport large numbers of people."

"It's very intimidating," muttered Jake.

"It's an Interstellar craft—can take you to the moon and beyond, no problem."

"To those supposedly secret bases on the far side?" questioned Harrison, only half serious.

"Certainly possible. Park the Skysaber over to the left. Give the 3200xi plenty of space."

"Good job," Jason said, as Jake positioned the *Skysaber* and powered down the toroidal plasma propulsion system. "You handled her nicely."

"I've had some practice," quipped Jake, not wanting to elaborate on his considerable flight time in the *Skysaber*.

"You sure you're ready to face your uncle? It could be ugly."

"No doubt it will be, but I can handle it. You guys ready? There's uniforms in the closet. You should be able to pass as workers. Just be sure to look like you know where you're going."

"We've studied the architectural drawings. We'll take some good video of what's going on in here. Otherwise, no one would believe us."

Jake grasped Jason by the arm and shook his hand. "Well, good luck, my friend . . . and I want to apologize for accusing you of spying."

Jason smiled. "No problem. I would have come to the same conclusion under the circumstances."

Harrison placed his arms on Jason's shoulders. "In my mind you're a real hero. There aren't many of your kind around today. And we sure need them."

Four levels exist in the Refuge Enclave underground city: Level 1 houses control systems, food production and offices. On Level 2 are located the retail stores, gardens, living quarters and railway station. Level 3 houses classrooms, health facilities, records, accounting and communication. The hangar is located on Level 3. On Level 4, the lowest level, is found shipping and receiving, storage and power generation.

Thinking it would be difficult to remain unnoticed on Level 1, Jake and Harrison started with Level 3. As they passed through the wide, well-lit corridors, they used their well-concealed eyeglass cameras to photograph every room with an open door or glass windows, taking care to avoid generating any special notice. As a cover, they pretended to be speaking to each other and taking notes to give the impression they were officials doing a survey of conditions.

The revelations started on Level 2. The elevator doors opened to reveal a vast cavernous space, filled with a plaza, a block of retail stores and a train station. "Shiiiit," whispered Harrison. "There is a whole damn village center down here. I can't believe it. And that train—it looks like one of those super-fast European types. Where does it go?"

"Probably to another underground city," suggested Jake.

Wasting no time, they walked toward an area with signage that read: "Food Supplies and Gardens." Jake and Harrison kept looking straight ahead, fearing that any unusual actions would indicate they were new to the area. Still, they found themselves constantly distracted by crowds of people moving between buildings, workers cleaning up the sidewalks, and the traffic on a two-lane road on which unmarked eighteen-wheelers traveled. They marveled at the detail, variety and size of the construction in which they found themselves.

Soon they noticed a low hum in the rooms and a slight breeze that moved through the space. And the lighting drew their interest: It gave the appearance of daylight complete with normal-looking shadows, but the shadows never moved.

Harrison whispered. "I'd like to find the power system. I'm curious as to how they're running this place."

"Let's check out the gardens first, I think we're almost there."

Turning a corner, they came upon several acres of mature gardens. Workers hustled back and forth, carrying tools, pushing wheelbarrows and dragging hoses. In the center of the garden area, a fountain gushed water. Harrison was amazed. "Will you look at that: tomatoes, broccoli, peas, corn, soybeans, greens . . . and herb gardens. Fresh food, lots of it. These people have it together."

"If you think about it: This is what you'd need to do if you wanted complete sustainability. Impressive. This is a serious operation."

Harrison grew somber. "Serious? Yeah, serious about the end of the world . . . Except it's *not* the end of the world for *their* select friends and families. But when they close the gates, those stuck outside are basically left behind to fight it out in a collapsing, climate-changing world. This sure doesn't make me feel good."

"Of course it's not fair, that's why we're taking these pictures."

"The folks here are not going to like it if their cover is blown."

"No they won't, but let's find the power station. We don't have much time."

Ten minutes later, the two men had descended to Level 4 and were examining a fenced-in area, behind which stood a massive set of four double toroidal-shaped structures, each thirty-feet wide and two-stories high. Power lines ran in several directions from a series of high-voltage transformers. "This is one big Universal Energy machine," remarked Harrison as he craned his neck, scanning horizontally back and forth across the complicated and elaborate elements of the power station. A hum emanated from the apparatus, and the cavern was ablaze with light. "Must be in the order of twenty to thirty megawatts, I'm guessing, to run everything in here. Boy, would I love to work with the guys who built this. Probably had help from the hybrids, don't you think?"

Jake continued to stare at the imposing and strangely-shaped structure. "I imagine they're here too. But look over there . . . it seems like that group of guys in uniforms is coming towards us . . . and they're walking fast. We'd better move along and make like we're busy finishing up our data collection."

CHAPTER FORTY

Jason's footsteps echoed off the hard, concrete walls. He found the hangar level eerily quiet and filled with a sullen, grey light. Exiting the building, he approached his car and notified his uncle of his imminent arrival by text message. Jason felt a sense of foreboding churning in his gut. Despite assurances to his newfound friends regarding his ability to prevail, Jason was fearful that the encounter would not go well. He wished he were thousands of miles away, but running from Garrett Henry was not an option.

After winding his way up the mountain, Jason parked in the circular drive fronting Garrett Henry's lodge overlooking the valley. So peaceful now, but not for long, he thought.

At the door, Jason was met by his uncle's housekeeper. "He's in the library," she intoned with a Spanish accent, apparently expecting him.

Jason entered the wood-paneled room. He noticed that several desk lamps were illuminated, necessitated by a darkening sky outside. Garrett Henry, wearing designer jeans and a grey silk shirt, was staring out through the large picture window, intentionally ignoring Jason's entrance.

"Hello, Uncle."

Garrett spun around to face Jason and strode toward the wide table that separated the two of them. He leaned on the tabletop, supporting himself with both hands. His voice dripped with venom.

"Your mother was a traitor, too. I never trusted her. When Malcolm wanted to bring her into the family I told him she was dangerous. She was too . . . *too* interested in do-goodism. She was always critical of our plans, and she had this thing about helping people. I told them it was a waste of time, just delaying the inevitable. He refused to believe me . . . said that he would continue to support her, despite her lack of support for our family's value system."

Jason came to her defense. "My mother really believed in what she was doing. She was trying to make things better."

"She took my brother with her. It was a stupid thing to do—taking that helicopter into the mountains—in the middle of winter—to measure glaciers. Who the hell cares about the glaciers? They're melting. So what? I told her it was too late to make a difference. They're doomed just like everyone downstream. But she didn't listen . . . and then the accident . . . So I took you in and I brought you up to become a full member of our family's financial empire."

Garrett Henry straightened up, his face twisted with fury. "Jason, I don't understand. I gave you the best education and training money can buy. And then you go and do this . . ."

Jason expected to take the first blows. "Of course, I appreciate what you've given me, but I've learned there's something more important in life than amassing money and things."

"Now you're sounding like your mother."

"I'll take that as a compliment."

"You'll get nothing more from our treasury. *Ever*."

"That treasury, as you refer to it, is not really yours to spend. It's just not right when only a few privileged families and individuals own and control most of the wealth on the planet. I couldn't let that stand, I had to do something to help restore the balance."

Garrett lowered his voice. He hissed with steely determination. "You and I both know there will be a reckoning. It's already begun. Our money and gold utilized appropriately is the only way humanity can survive the collapse." He looked up, staring into the high ceiling supported with large pine logs and skillful carpentry. "When the ship is sinking and you don't have sufficient lifeboats, you exercise triage: You're forced to choose who goes and who doesn't. We've made our choice. We have the power to make that choice."

Jason sensed his own anger building. "Who's to say *you* or *we* deserve a seat in the lifeboat? There are a lot of people out there who deserve a place as well."

Garrett smiled with evil confidence. "It's the Golden Rule: 'He who has the gold, makes the rules.' That's just the way it is. We can do what we want."

And then he frowned. "There's no money in basic lives. If you're not productive and can't pay, we don't want you around— it's as simple as that. And I will remind you—no one has the power to stop us. Sure, that theft of $15 trillion is a blow, but it will not prevent us from achieving our long-term goals."

Jason was quick to respond, releasing the anger that had been brewing in his belly. "Don't be so sure. You may be bent on achieving world domination and creating your breakaway civilization, but you don't understand how many strong and committed people are rising to face the challenges of the world."

Jason paused and inhaled deeply, formulating his next words. He was intent on speaking from his heart—something he had never before done with his uncle. He was pushing the envelope. Fixing his eyes on Garrett, he let it fly: "They're not selfish and self-centered like you and your covert cadre of monetary hoarders. They understand the power of love and generosity, and they want what's best for the greater good. That's the world I want to belong to."

Garrett stepped closer to Jason. His eyes bore down, seeking to intimidate Jason into submission. "*I* will determine the world you will belong to and it will not be a world of naïve, emotional do-gooders. You've betrayed the trust that our family and I have placed in you. That is unforgivable. You'll be banished to a remote outpost that I've established to deal with people who have compromised our security and threatened our mission."

Garrett stepped over to a desk where an electronic tablet lay, its screen lit with an indistinguishable graphic. He touched it, registering a command. He turned back to Jason, his voice thick with disappointment, "You'll be joined in your exile with a number of upstart photosynthesizers who are attempting to defy our directives. They won't survive long without sunlight and water. You'll also have as company two of your unlucky companions we've just detained. And just to let you know—you're entitled to no recourse and no appeal. You have only yourself to blame."

The door opened and a tall man appeared flanked by two security guards. Garrett gave the order. "Zechn, please escort this man to the holding area and include him in the transshipment to Area Z."

Garrett Henry turned his back to Jason and returned to stare out the window. The two security guards grabbed Jason by his arms and pulled him forcibly from the room. Jason offered no resistance.

CHAPTER FORTY ONE

Lake Albion Valley
Photosynthesizer's compound

Debbie Chen had called together the leadership team. A half-dozen men and women, all displaying green-tinted skin, occupied a small room behind the kitchen and eating area. The plan was simple: have everyone leave the area *en masse*. So far, it had been difficult to attract public attention to their plight. However, several young men had recently fled the compound and had managed to pass on critical information to the provincial authorities. Whether or not help would come from the outside in time to support their rebellion, no one could know for sure. As far as Debbie Chen could tell, they were alone and on their own. That was until her attention was directed to a nearby window where a noisy, hawk-like bird was insistently scratching on the glass. "He seems to have something in his mouth," an alert observer noted.

Debbie excused herself from the group and stepped outside. She walked around the building, taking care to avoid attracting attention. As soon as she was within sight of the bird, she gestured to the raptor with a wave of her hand to approach her in the shielded area, away from the windows. The bird perched on a low wall next to Debbie and offered the small piece of paper to her. She opened it and smiled, whispering to herself, "They're here, help is on the way!"

The note asked for information regarding the current state of affairs and how best to enter the compound unnoticed. Debbie removed a pen from her shirt pocket and drew an arrow indicating the location of a service entrance next to their compound. She also noted: *Several trucks have been acquired. People are ready to leave. Need some kind of diversion. Be creative. DC.*

Folding up the note, she offered it to the bird. His beak wrapped around it. Woman and bird relished the moment as if they recognized each other. Though in different kinds of bodies, they shared common cause and a common bond.

The raptor ascended into the air with a flush of rapidly beating wings. It made its way through the tall pines and was soon absorbed by the gathering darkness. Debbie, empowered by a set of new possibilities, returned to the meeting. The group sensed something had changed when they observed Debbie's more determined stride and the confidence in her face.

"I just received a message that help is coming. We need to act normally, as if nothing is happening."

A middle-aged man expressed his concern. "That's reassuring, but I think they know we're up to something. We've got to act soon."

"I agree," said Debbie, "but not yet. As far as they know, we're just preparing for our regular quarterly meeting to elect our internal supervisors."

"Have you seen the weather outside?" asked another. "Looks to me like a major storm is brewing. Maybe this isn't such a good time to try and leave."

"Weather can be our ally," Debbie replied.

A murmur of agreement rolled up from the group.

"There's Razr," exclaimed Ariel pointing through the windshield of the van. "He's back."

Snapdragon and Catherine watched the bird fly into the trees beyond them. Ariel stepped back into the rear compartment of the camper van and opened the sliding door. Within minutes, Razr stepped forward out of the trees to meet his co-conspirators.

He handed the note to Snapdragon.

"We'll need to create a diversion. Catherine, you drive while I set up the conditions for confusion."

Catherine soon had the van back on the road. Snapdragon initiated a digital program intended to introduce a series of error messages into the communication stream between the mountain control center and the security forces stationed around the compound.

"Pass by the compound," Snapdragon ordered, "and we'll turn off onto the service road. Then we'll get to work. We'll go on foot. Ariel, give us an update on what's going on inside. Use your remote viewing."

As the van made its way down the highway, Ariel closed her eyes and focused mentally. Razr watched her face as it tightened and relaxed repeatedly. A strained expression played across her face. "What's wrong?" he asked.

"I'm seeing activity at the mountain . . . at the command center there. Garrett Henry is giving an order to surround the photosynthesizer's compound. 'If they try anything, shoot to kill,' he's saying to them. I can't believe it. How can he be so ruthless? We've got to warn them."

"No, we've got to get them out of there," said Catherine.

Snapdragon handed Ariel an electronic tablet. "Draw me a picture of the layout of the compound and any adjoining buildings. You used to live there, right?"

"Yes. I'm pretty familiar with the area."

Ariel began moving her fingers across the glass surface of the tablet, drawing a series of squares, circles and lines. She indicated which buildings were located inside the compound and which were outside.

Snapdragon got the picture immediately. "What's this large garage-like building outside the compound?"

"Maintenance. Vehicle and equipment maintenance."

"Perfect target. We'll place combustion grenades around the building. I can ignite them remotely. That's how we'll create a diversion. Anybody in there now?"

Ariel closed her eyes. "No. It's empty."

"Good. We want to avoid harming any of the workers or staff."

Catherine began to slow the van. "Here's the service road. No one's here."

"Turn in," said Snapdragon.

"Look," said Catherine. "There's two trucks down there with guards."

"Drive into the trees and park. Everybody ready?"

Catherine pulled the van into a cluster of trees. As the side door of the van was opened, a jet-black panther leapt from the vehicle and disappeared into the woods that separated the compound from the lake. Minutes later, three women dressed in hiker's clothing and carrying small backpacks were working their way through the woods and circling around to the maintenance building.

Snapdragon, carrying a small satchel, skirted the compound until she reached the service entrance gate. Observing that the gate was unguarded, she removed a pressurized can of ultra-cold liquid from her satchel, which she sprayed on the lock. It was frozen to -100°F in seconds. She then hit it hard with a hammer she had removed from her pack. The gate lock opened instantly. She replaced the damaged lock to make it appear functional. She continued along the periphery of the compound to check on Catherine and Ariel. Jogging through the woods, she caught glimpses of the panther occasionally running alongside her. The forest was alive with the murmurings of various animals. Apparently, the panther was rallying the animals just in case wildlife reinforcements might be needed.

The three women met up behind an old well house fifty feet from the compound peripheral fence—a six-foot-high security barrier with barbed wire on top. "Looks like they really don't want people leaving," noted Catherine."

Snapdragon turned to Ariel and Catherine, "Did you set the charges?"

"We did," replied Catherine, "but there were people around the front so we couldn't position any there."

"That's okay. We only need three or four to ignite to create a lot of fire and smoke. Let's move inside the compound and get everyone organized."

The three women moved through the woods, carefully avoiding detection by security personnel. They slipped through the service entrance gate and entered the compound. The occupants were stunned when they recognized the familiar faces of the visitors. Snapdragon quickly cautioned everyone to silence their reactions. A young woman led the trio to Debbie Chen, who embraced Snapdragon in an emotional hug. As Snapdragon and Debbie Chen looked deeply into each other's eyes, Catherine was struck by the beauty of the contrasting colors on the two women's faces: warm brown and forest green. Sensing the urgency, Debbie led Catherine, Snapdragon and Ariel into a small meeting room filled with photosynthesizers. The crowd immediately erupted in cheers and spontaneous applause. Ariel's eyes sparkled as she scanned the room. For the moment, her fear regarding the tumultuous events occurring outside the building was erased.

Debbie Chen was the first to speak. "We have a plan. Everyone needs to be ready to move out. My friends have set up a diversion. That should distract the security guards. We'll leave through the service entrance which is now unlocked. We've got several trucks outside. We're going to bust out of here . . . *finally.*" Debbie turned to Snapdragon. "How much time do we have?"

"Maybe twenty minutes?"

"Okay, everyone, get ready. Let's do it," Debbie shouted to the crowd.

In ten minutes, the forty or so residents of the facility had filled the room with shoulder bags, small suitcases and duffels. The group waited quietly, wearing rain jackets and hats suspecting that they would soon be dealing with a major weather event. The air in the room was charged with anticipation and high anxiety.

Snapdragon removed a monitoring device from her satchel and placed it on a nearby table. She activated it, plugging in a set of earphones to listen in on the communication stream. A shadow passed over her face. "What's wrong?" asked Debbie Chen who was sitting next to her.

"There on to us. They're sending additional security personnel down here—and we think they have orders to kill."

"Then we need to leave now."

"I'll trigger the grenades. Get your people ready to move out."

Debbie leapt up from the table and Snapdragon activated her remote device. In the background could be heard a series of muffled explosions.

"It's started," said Catherine with a sober finality.

The group grabbed their packs and started moving out. Sirens could be heard in the distance becoming louder. Ignoring the sounds, Snapdragon and Debbie led the group toward the service gate. As they reached the door, Ariel stopped them. "Wait! I see a whole group of men with assault weapons waiting outside for us. Let's not give them a reason to gun us down."

"Then we're trapped," said Debbie. "What now?"

A loud clap of thunder drowned out the end of Debbie's sentence. A deluge of rain began. All eyes rose to the ceiling of the building, as the rooftop drumming increased in volume. The anxiety in the room continued to build. Catherine turned to Ariel, Debbie and Snapdragon. She said, "We sing."

CHAPTER FORTY TWO

The rain became a torrential fury. The ground absorbed the first few inches, but the water sought streambeds that, in turn, quickly overflowed and flooded the landscape. Forest fires had previously denuded the hillsides above the valley, causing the ground to harden from the extreme heat generated by the fires. This prevented the soil from absorbing water. As a result, the liquid onslaught morphed into waves of rock and mud, which rushed down the mountainside, scouring away anything that stood in its way.

In the underground operations center, rivulets of water began to seep into its interior. The wily liquid trickled into rooms and corridors, finding its way through cracks in walls. The water slid like a snake across floors and stealthily infiltrated ceiling tiles. Workers stared at ever-accelerating ceiling drips and dodged expanding pools of liquid that crept along any flat, floor surface.

Warning lights flashed on heating and ventilation control consoles. Operators barked instructions to technicians to close outside vents and gates. As workers responded, the hallways rang with the clang of vents sealing and workers shouting to one another. Panic filled the air.

"Seems like they've got a problem on their hands," Harrison said to Jake as they sat on the floor in a holding area with a dozen other middle-aged men and women. Four guards in camouflage military uniforms holding assault rifles stood menacingly over them. Jake and Harrison had already ascertained that the other men and women beside them had been attempting to leave the underground city without authorization. The prisoners remained silent, intently listening to the buzzing of alarms and the trembling of the walls around them.

The door opened and a heavy-set guard barked, "Everyone up and start moving. No talking."

The captives raised themselves to their feet. Their hands and feet had been left unshackled so they could sit and stand without assistance. The guards trained their weapons on the captives as the men proceeded out the door and into the corridor. In the hanger area, additional guards positioned beneath the ARV-3200xi directed the prisoners to board the black circular craft, its running lights illuminated and its hatch and stairway open. One by one, the captives ascended the stairway and entered into the waiting craft.

Despite his concern about what would happen next, Jake was curious about the ARV-3200xi. Expecting a plush, elegant interior, like inside the *Skysaber*, Jake was disappointed to see that this ship's interior was purely functional. It was designed as a no-frills, economy class transport with unadorned metal walls and basic coach-style seats, set close together to accommodate the maximum number of people in a given space. Jake and Harrison prepared to take their seats along with their companions.

As they approached the seating area, Jake and Harrison were forcibly bumped by man who emerged unnoticed from the side of the room. They stepped aside as a courtesy and recognized a familiar face: It was Jason. He winked at them, displaying a contrived scowl mixed with a half-smile of recognition. As the room remained in confusion and the noise of the shuffling of feet continued, Jason positioned himself between Harrison and Jake. He leaned toward both of them, acting as if he was losing his balance, but in fact was whispering in their ears: "As soon as we're airborne, the ship will take a series of sharp dives and turns intended to knock the guards off their feet. At that time we'll relieve the guards of their weapons. Each of us should sit close to a guard. I'll take the one in front; Jake, you take the guy in back, and Harrison, you take the one on the side." Jason then handed Jake and Harrison some plastic wire wraps. "When you've got the weapons, ask for help in securing their hands with the tie wraps."

Jason, Jake and Harrison picked seats on the aisle next to the three standing guards. Nervously, they waited as the final prisoners were loaded, several guards departed the ship, and the hatch was closed. A low hum signaled that the craft was preparing to move across the hangar deck and into the sky beyond. Jake and Harrison could only guess at its destination. Their attention, though, was fully focused on the immediate task at hand: successfully overpowering their captors.

They did not have long to wait. As the craft exited the hangar, it sloped up steeply and banked sharply to the side, throwing all the guards to the floor like rocks in a tumbler. Jake, Jason and Harrison leapt to their feet and rushed to grab the rifles now clattering across the floor. The other prisoners immediately responded in kind and threw themselves at the flailing guards. Within seconds, the former prisoners had overwhelmed their captors and were now in control of the situation. Jason tossed tie-wraps to the others to fasten the hands of the guards tightly behind their backs.

Jason shouted, "Nice work. Looks like we're in charge now."

"But who's in charge of the ship?" Jake asked Jason. "Must be someone you know, I assume."

"His name is Zechn Reu, a hybrid. My uncle considered him to be one of his most trusted associates."

"So what changed his mind?"

"I think knowing Ariel had an effect. Remarkable woman, really."

"She is. And speaking of her, we've got to find out what's happening at the compound. They might require our help. We need to meet with the Captain."

The four men climbed the short set of stairs and arrived at the spacious bridge of the ARV 3200xi. Jake marveled at the complexity and elegance of the control consoles and the detail of the many graphic displays mounted on the walls and above compact desk surfaces. He could see the ship was equipped with an array of special features designed for long-distance travel. Jake could easily imagine the craft ferrying its passengers to far-away planets and distant star systems.

Jason introduced Harrison and Jake to Zechn Reu. Jake recognized Zechn as the pilot who had taken over control of the *Skysaber* from him at the secret military base in Nevada. "So we meet again," Jake said warmly as he shook Zechn's hand.

"This time over more favorable circumstances, I believe."

Jake decided to broaden the relationship. "I think you know Ariel Connelly."

"I do, she and I have gotten to know each other—actually quite well."

"Can we use the ship to provide assistance to the people at the compound?"

"My flight plan directs me to make a pickup there—more prisoners, I've been told."

Jason interrupted the conversation. "But first I need to return to the mountain; I've left something important there."

"What's that?" asked Jake.

"Can't you guess? The *Skysaber.*"

Jake smiled. "Of course, it's your ship."

"I know where to go and I can avoid the guards."

Jason turned to Zechn. "Can you drop me off on the top of the mountain? Over the emergency exit tunnel. I should be able to work my way back to the hangar . . . that is, if it's not flooded too badly."

"Or worse, collapsed," warned Zechn.

"I have to try. That ship means a lot to me, and I think she can be very useful to our future projects."

Jake took note of Jason's statement of personal commitment to the cause.

"You're a good man, Jason," Harrison said warmly.

Jason's face betrayed a hint of embarrassment and he looked away. His mother and father's faces flashed through his mind and he felt at peace. This was a new feeling. All his life, he'd been haunted by the sense that working for his uncle was taking him further and further away from what was truly important. Now, perhaps, he had found his calling.

"We're over the mountain," Zechn announced. "I'm seeing massive mudslides. Some of them have washed away buildings—take a look."

The men rushed toward the viewing window. Zechn had slowed the craft to 10 mph, hovering over the ground at an altitude of 2,000 feet. Despite the rain, the clouds were high enough and the light sufficient to allow them to view the entire valley. In the distance, they noted flames lighting up the sky over the photosynthesizer's compound. Jake pointed out the worrisome development to Harrison. "Looks like there's trouble over there."

Jason, though, was intent on locating his uncle's home along the top edge of the mountain, already scarred by mudslides. "Hold this line, Zechn," Jason called out. "Fly over my uncle's house on the ridge."

Zechn brought the ship over the spot where he thought the house was located. Jason's voice weakened with apparent grief. "All I can see is a pile of rubble, sliding down the side of the mountain. That *was* my uncle's house."

Zechn stared at the men, curious about how they were handling their emotions. He always found it fascinating how human relationships seemed to change dramatically when placed under stress or experiencing loss. As half human, half ET, Zechn had some understanding intellectually of this behavior, but he always experienced a reluctance to yield to such feelings himself.

Zechn guided the craft away from the ridge and back toward the mountain refuge.

"Look," said Jason, "we're over the airport area and . . . well, would you look at that . . . "

Jake and Harrison stared down at the broad runway. "I see a private jet attempting to take off," noted Jake. "But it's going to have a hard time in weather this dangerous."

"It's a Gulfstream 650. It's my uncle's plane, and it looks like he's leaving."

"Probably a good time to get down there," suggested Zechn as he positioned the craft over the underground city.

Jason filled a backpack with basic supplies and bid his friends good luck. Entering the exit chamber, Zechn activated the transporter beam to lower Jason into a small clearing inside a cluster of trees. Surrounded by darkness and pummeled by rain, Jason was now alone and on his own.

CHAPTER FORTY THREE

Inside the photosynthesizer's compound

"Sing?" The group was confused.

"Yes, to the water," Catherine said, raising her voice so all could hear. "We sing to the lake and the rain. We call upon the water to work with us. Close your eyes; touch the water inside you with your mind and heart and start singing. Do it now!"

A girl child began to hum a simple and compelling tune. The song sounded strangely ancient and yet profoundly familiar. Others joined in and the air began to shimmer. The diversity of voices, male and female, young and old, produced stunning harmonies, which lifted everyone and the room into a resonant realm of palpable enchantment. The multi-layered sound began to move beyond the building, into the woods, and across the placid surface of the lake.

At first, nothing appeared to be happening. But along the lakeshore, the panther had gathered deer, muskrats, coyotes, rabbits, and birds. The animals and birds began adding their own vocalizations to the magical melody emanating from the building. And then the extraordinary occurred: The lake surface came alive. Consorting with the steady rain, it pulsed back and forth as the tonal vibrations penetrated its clear waters. Then very slowly, the lake commenced exhaling a series of ghost-like images. Phantom shapes of long-extinct animals emerged from the undulating surface of the water—an apparent release of evolutionary memories held in molecular secret by the water for millions of years. Mastodons, saber-tooth tigers, camels, giant bears, six-foot-wide flying reptiles, creatures of the fantasy worlds of ages long ago began ascending into the sky above the lake. The present-day, wild creatures gathered alongside the lake and stared in wonder, sensing faint recognition of their ancient ancestors.

As the lake released the phantasmagoric menagerie, the rain slowed its assault upon the compound. To their surprise, the militia suddenly found themselves staring at an assortment of indescribable creatures with rows of razor-sharp teeth bared and flashing, hurtling toward them from the sky. Not sure whether or not the horrid apparitions were real or imagined, the security team decided to flee to the safety of their vehicles. Astoundingly, the variety of specters seemed to have no end, descending from all directions in a nightmare of chaos combined with archaic roars and cries of terrifying intensity.

"Stay focused and keep singing," Catherine reminded the group, as the unearthly sounds penetrated the building, causing heartbeats to quicken. "Just follow our directions."

Debbie and Snapdragon ran into the room. "The coast is clear, the armed men are gone. Bring your things. Now!"

Reluctantly, the group set out into the rain, the air around them blackened by the storm. Brilliant lightning bolts and the accompanying ear-splitting thunder claps caused some to cry out. As the straggling, soaked escapees reached the area where they expected to find their get-away vehicles, they stopped, frozen in disappointment.

"My God," said Debbie Chen. "They've destroyed all the trucks. We're stranded."

Ariel realized that it would only be a matter of time before the militia would descend on them with guns blazing—an outcome she immediately rejected from her mind. I need to send out an emergency rescue call, she ordered herself. Ariel stepped away from the confusion and panic that was now overtaking the group despite Catherine's efforts to encourage calm.

As Ariel searched for refuge from the rain and chaos, the panther appeared, glanced at her and assertively turned into the forest. Ariel followed the feline into a cluster of trees thick enough to protect her from the rain's driving force. Just beyond the trees, Ariel could see a large empty field of short, brown grasses. Closing her eyes, she sent out her psychic interrogator beam, requesting immediate transportation aid. Surprisingly, her head stung with an almost instant response. It was Zechn Reu. *Have available transport. Approaching the compound now. Will land in nearby field. Have people ready for boarding.*

Ariel took immediate action. Sprinting, she returned to the group and discovered the panther had assembled a diverse collection of local animals, which had, in turn, surrounded the photosynthesizers in a circle of support.

"Follow me," Ariel yelled at the top of her voice. "We're going to be rescued."

Catherine, working with Debbie Chen to preserve order, relaxed her guard as a wave of deep emotion flowed over her. She was so proud of her daughter, but there was no time to reflect. Springing into action, Catherine ordered those closest to her to move quickly. As the group pressed forward, the panther circled once and bounded alongside Ariel as she led the stragglers through the forest and towards the nearby field. A bright light could be seen flashing through the wind-whipped treetops, revealing a huge circular shape moving over the forest canopy.

As the bewildered refugees approached the edge of the field, powerful beacons from the descending ship illuminated the ground. "Let's get the group into the ship as fast as possible!" ordered Snapdragon, brushing her rain-soaked hair away from her face.

"Look," cried Catherine.

The three turned their attention to the field where the craft had landed. Inviting lights radiated warmly from the deployed stairway. Jake and Harrison were running through the rain towards the escapees with their hands gesturing, "Come quickly." The rumble of approaching motors could be heard in the distance. No one thought them friendly.

"Everyone this way!" shouted Debbie Chen, as she led the haggard group toward the welcoming lights that led into the belly of the huge ARV-3200xi. While racing to reach the craft, some slipped on the wet grass, only to be immediately lifted up by their companions and pulled forward. All helped to continue the rapid loading process. As they reached the underside of the ship, the refugees would breathe a sigh of relief as the ship's body protected them from the pummeling rain. Snapdragon held back and removed a remote device from her satchel. Inputting a code, she detonated an explosion in the distance—the RV. She was always careful about covering up her tracks and making it as difficult as possible for opponents to access her unique technology.

Catherine was the first up the entrance ramp and joined Harrison to facilitate the seating of the soggy group. Jake assisted people to find storage for their packs and suitcases. Debbie and Snapdragon stood beside the ramp, scanning the forest with expert eyes, hoping not to see trucks suddenly emerge out of the woods. Finally, as the last few people boarded, Ariel peered anxiously across the field, searching for a feline form. At the last possible moment, the panther came bounding across the wet ground, and in one powerful leap was on the ramp and sliding into the ship. The ramp retracted with a *thunk,* and the ARV-3200xi ascended rapidly with a burst of antigravity propulsion and vanished into the storm. Seconds later, the field was blasted with several blinding pulses of lightning followed by a series of thunderous claps. A dozen armored vehicles invaded the field and an army of men leapt out, rifles raised and ready to fire.

They stared at an empty, waterlogged landscape.

CHAPTER FORTY FOUR

Inside the ARV-3200xi, the exhausted passengers were filled with a sense of profound relief. Most everyone escaped without injury, and they were now free to chart a course for their own future. Switching to dry clothes was the first order of business. Wet pants, shirts and socks hung on every available protrusion. The ARV-3200xi was beginning to take on the appearance of a refugee transport ship. Indeed, as future history would record, this was but the first of many of its climate change refugee airlifts.

Once the group of photosynthesizers felt they had the situation under control, Catherine and Debbie Chen approached Zechn Reu. Catherine observed that Zechn had slightly vertical eyes that betrayed a distinctly otherworldly presence. His demeanor spoke of distant and cool, understated strength. Zechn anticipated their question: "Do you have a destination in mind?"

Debbie Chen had been appointed to speak for the group of photosynthesizers. "We have forty people who need access to special facilities—good light, water, and space to grow spirulina, greens and vegetables. Some of our people are originally from different photosynthesizer groups."

"This is what we'll do," said Zechn. "There's a photosynthesizer community in New Mexico. I'll drop everyone off there. Your people can decide later if they want to go somewhere else."

"That will work," said Debbie graciously.

Debbie Chen left to inform the group of the decision. She knew they'd be thrilled to hear the news.

Jake had been restraining his curiosity. "Now that the business of who goes where is settled, I have to ask: Just who are you working for now? Garrett Henry or someone else?"

Ariel was taken aback by Jake's brusque comment. Zechn replied with a patient ease. "Let me explain. As part of a secret program promulgated by Garrett Henry, chlorophyll-metabolized humans, or photosynthesizers as you refer to them, are viewed as highly desirable workers. As you know, they can generate much of their own food energy from light, simple nutrients and water, and they're less inclined to making trouble—excepting Ariel."

Ariel smiled with evident pride.

Catherine was curious about his comment. "Of course I understand the energy thing, but 'less inclined to making trouble?' Could you explain?"

"It's been observed that the photosynthesizers have either adopted or acquired—it's not quite understood yet—a more peaceful mental and physical nature. It seems they're happiest growing their own food and developing deep personal and intellectual connections with their fellow photosynthesizers. Their skills are of the highest and most sophisticated order, and they commonly abhor violence."

Zechn paused and silently conveyed the impression that he was about to mention something very important. "This makes them a special kind of human, a prime candidate for something Ariel and I and certain others refer to as 'Human 3.0.'"

"3.0?" asked Catherine, glancing toward Ariel, who was sitting nearby. "I've not heard anything about it."

"It's the idea that we—the photosynthesizers, the hybrids and sympathetic others—can create a better world together," said Ariel. "The world we envision is one based on peaceful, simple living and recognizing the commonality of all life—earth-based and otherwise. This is the world we want to create—Human 3.0." Ariel grinned confidently.

Zechn continued to explain that he and others like himself have been biding their time, playing along with those who have dominated human finance, politics, economics and the various militaries for centuries, waiting for the appropriate time to intervene in the public course of human affairs.

"Let's hope the timing is right," said Jake, struggling between doubt and hope.

"Nothing is assured," said Zechn. "Major uncertainties exist, but the rules of the game have now been changed."

CHAPTER FORTY FIVE

Zechn set a course for the American Southwest. The ARV-3200xi skipped across the dry landscapes of eastern Washington, paralleled the dark Bitterroot Range in Idaho, slipped over the grey blur of the Great Salt Lake in Utah and slowed so its passengers could marvel over the yawning vermillion abyss of Arizona's Grand Canyon, bathed in dawn's early light.

As the craft turned eastward, the ship's passengers found themselves entranced by the tall sandstone sentinels that stood astride the ochre Arizona landscape. On the desert floor, a lone Navajo sheepherder guarding his flock tracked the sun-glinting disc sailing across the turquoise skyline. The wind-weathered man wondered about the ship's occupants, its destination and purpose. He felt no surprise, however, as such sightings of aerial phenomena were common in this land of spirit and otherworldly happenings.

Easily spotted from the air were the tall, landscape-dominating smokestacks of giant coal-fired, power-generating stations. These air-pollution machines were now finally stilled, as Universal Energy power rendered them mothballed combustion museums.

Water is extremely rare here. No flowing rivers or year-round streams exist. Instead, the residents of these mystic mesas have learned how to pray the water from the sky and draw lingering groundwater from the sand. The historic longevity of the communities that have thrived on this land is testimony to their ancient rituals and deep, natural wisdom.

The arid land over which the craft flew soon became dotted with a network of road scars and denuded areas. The raw etchings on the landscape were the results of destructive gas and oil drilling. Tens of millions of gallons of carcinogen-infused waters had been forced into the ground to shock and shatter the delicate web of soil and rock, to suck yet more barrels of carbon-heavy fossil fuels into the daylight. Constant truck traffic and the roar of compressors and pumps had long violated the precious peacefulness of these sacred lands, long-treasured by Native Americans. Lurid flames of yellow, angry methane alight had soiled the formerly ink-black, star-studded night-skies. Now the drilling had ceased and the methane flames had been permanently extinguished.

Working its way east, the ARV-3200xi passed over the spectacular, abandoned settlement of Chaco Canyon. This mysterious complex of skillfully-set stone speaks of advanced architectural technology undertaken during the 9th to 13th centuries. The design and intention at Chaco Canyon still defies the most inquisitive of archeology sleuths. Its central village, crafted into a stunning D-shape of multi-stories and circular ceremonial chambers, suggests to the imagination a kind of earth-bound starship. One is tempted to ask if ancient sky travelers had a hand in the design and construction of the baffling structures that exist throughout the canyon. From the air, these structures uncannily resemble printed electronic circuit boards.

Leaving the land of the Ancient Ones, the ship approached the Jemez Mountains of New Mexico. The mountain itself is all that remains from two unfathomably-large volcanic eruptions that spread pulverized debris as far east as Oklahoma 1.1 and 1.6 million years ago. Its peak, 11,258 feet high, is considered sacred by the local Pueblo People. It overlooks a broad, twenty-mile-wide crater, carpeted in lush green grasses during the summer months and full of silent snowfields in winter. It was this grand caldera that the ARV-3200xi sought as its next destination.

The craft settled down into a wide meadow bordered by ponderosa pines. It was filled with a settlement of familiar greenhouses, which included a recently-built campus of energy-efficient buildings. As passengers began to disembark, Catherine recognized a familiar face.

Catherine's close friend Petra Harcourt rushed to meet her. Petra had inexplicably disappeared during the incendiary attack on their village, Tierra de la Luz, in the Pecos Mountains of New Mexico several years before.

The two women virtually collided with each other, embracing and rocking back and forth with hugs. Catherine could restrain her curiosity no longer: "Petra, what happened to you?"

Avoiding a verbal response, Petra pulled Catherine out of the line of passengers departing from the ship. She led Catherine away from the gathering crowd. "I had to get out of there fast and remain out of sight. I knew too much and had too much experience with the algae technology. The Homeland Security people knew that so they looked high and low for me."

"But they had us surrounded. How did you avoid them?"

"I was tipped off ahead of time . . . by guess who?"

Catherine took a wild guess. "Akkens?"

Petra grasped Catherine's hand. "Yes. Too much was at stake. He told me I had to be available to restart the experiment away from the control of Homeland Security and the corporate guys. He was afraid the science we were developing would fall into the wrong hands and he just didn't want that to happen. I was his 'Plan B—the evolutionary wild card,' as he put it."

"I have to give that guy a lot of credit, but I could never tell whose side he was on."

"He had to play it that way."

"So how did you end up back here?"

"Well, of course, my brother Steve is here—in Los Alamos. He hid me in a cabin until the Homeland Security people left the state. Akkens went to Nevada to set up the program there. After a few months in hiding, I thought the coast was clear."

"And what about Jonathan?"

"He was taken to a different military base, somewhere back East. He's helping to set up a photosynthesis operation there."

Petra went on to explain how the Los Alamos Laboratory had been rebooted as the International Center for Appropriate Technology. Federal funding had poured in to develop a major algae research program that included a state-of-the-art greenhouse, photo-bioreactor production area and laboratory. Petra's personal experience with cultivating spirulina and developing a human photosynthesis project deemed her highly valuable asset as the lab planned to establish a replicate program. Though it was initially considered classified, word got out when a few green people were seen in town. However, the communities around Los Alamos are pretty good at keeping secrets, as they've had lots of practice since the days of the Manhattan Project. As the photosynthesis community grew, Petra insisted it be moved to the caldera for safety and privacy.

Petra's face lit up, her ebullience was now at full throttle. "But you're here; you're back, Ariel's back, Debbie Chen, Jake, Harrison, Snapdragon, and Razr—the whole damn dream team. . . How long can you stay?"

Catherine was not sure how to answer. Thoughts of the Colorado Mountains, of her animal tracking projects, of people and places that had meant so much to her, tumbled through her mind. Those thoughts and sensations collided with her profound experiences in the Midwest, with the ACJC and the Great Lakes Water Gathering. And, of course, the need to confront the extraordinary challenges of a rapidly changing world was never far from her mind. Then, too, she had to consider her feelings for Jake. Her heart was confused, preventing her from arriving at a clear decision.

Catherine ventured a response. "So much has happened since then. I can't believe it's been just a couple of years since those first conversations. But I feel I'm needed back in the Midwest at the

American Climate Justice Collaborative—the ACJC has some major funding now, enough to make a real difference in the world."

"Well then, you've got your work cut out for you. I can understand. But before you leave, there's someone I want you to meet."

Catherine followed Petra into the log and stone office building. As they walked down the narrow hallway, Catherine noted the sign "Lab" on the door. Petra opened the door and invited Catherine to step inside. She recognized the man working inside—an older scientist dressed in a white lab coat. "Ah, Dr. Connelly. So good to see you again."

Catherine was at a loss for words, but mustered up a reply. "You're always full of surprises, Dr. Akkens. I just never know where you'll turn up next, but I've seen that you've certainly done much to advance the science of human photosynthesis."

"Why thank you for the compliment. And I must tell you that your early arguments and personal commitment to the cause strongly influenced me—actually changing the way I thought about the world."

Catherine found Akkens' words personally encouraging and calming. They strengthened her resolution to return to the ACJC. She knew that the clock was ticking and the challenges were mounting. The fuse was lit and it was a short fuse. And there was something else, someone dear to her whom she needed to visit before she returned to Lake Michigan's shores.

CHAPTER FORTY SIX

"Petra, I need to visit with your brother. Where can I find him?"

"He's in town. Steve often talks about you . . ." Petra's voice trailed off in a way that hinted of subtle encouragement. "Give him a call."

Catherine was soon on the road in a borrowed car winding her way along the narrow two-lane, cliff-hugging road to the fabled town of Los Alamos, about fifteen miles away.

Once a home to Ancestral Puebloan residents, the mountain fortress known as the Los Alamos National Laboratory had accumulated a modern history of scientific activities, both dramatic and deadly. Since 1917, the site had served as a base for an elite boys' school, which in 1942 became overrun by the U.S. military in its frantic quest to create the world's first atomic bomb. As a young man, J. Robert Oppenheimer found the mountains of New Mexico a welcome retreat where he would disappear for days on horseback. When he was tapped to direct the American effort to build The Bomb, Oppenheimer selected the remote Jemez Mountain plateau as the ideal place to sequester the world's most brilliant scientific minds. As history records, these sorcerers of science successfully harnessed the physics of matter, and in the words of Dr. Oppenheimer, ". . . became death and the destroyer of worlds."

As Catherine approached Steve McDonald's two-story, wood-frame home, she was fraught with emotions. She had history with

Steve: They had grown up together, both obsessed with science. As children, they would catch insects and track animals in nearby forests, and their parents would search for them at dinnertime, usually finding them in a tool shed poring through science textbooks and excitedly discussing potential research projects. Catherine chose wildlife biology and Steve a career in forestry. Their early friendship generated an emotional connection that ran soul-deep. After marrying others and suffering divorces, a lingering sense of missed opportunity continued to haunt them both. Catherine knew she was tempting that dormant, heart-based attraction by choosing to meet with her old friend. Still, she could not imagine leaving the area without a visit.

"Cath, so good to see you again," Steve said, his eyes sparkling, stepping forward to embrace her. She willingly opened to his arms and they held each other longer than either expected. As they reluctantly stepped back, Steve invited Catherine into his living room. "What are you doing here?"

Catherine was alarmed at Steve's physical appearance. The grooves on his face had deepened and his grey hair had become more transparent since she had last seen him two years ago. She wondered what had caused the accelerated aging. For the moment, she filed the thought.

"It's a long story. I visited with Petra up at the caldera, but I couldn't leave without checking in with you—just to see what you're up to."

"I'm so glad. Say, it's a beautiful, sunny day. Let's go for a hike. I'll make some sandwiches. It'll be a good chance to catch up. There are things happening here. Can I swear you to secrecy? I'm not kidding—this is important stuff. You're one of the few people I can share this with."

Catherine felt the rush of old memories flashing through her mind's eye, but this seemed far more serious. "Of course."

A few miles outside of town, they pulled into a parking lot next to the trail that led to the remains of a prehistoric cliff-side village. The trail followed a narrow pathway that wound up and through the grey volcanic tuff, a dusty material that covered much of the area and comprised the cliffs above them. Over the years of human habitation, the tuff had been worn down by the footsteps of many generations of men, women and children, allowing visitors to literally walk in the same crevices as the Ancestral Puebloan people did so long ago.

"This is spectacular," Catherine remarked as she reveled in the magnificent view of the broad valley below. It spanned the distance between the Jemez Mountain mesas where she stood and the Sangre de Cristo Mountain Range that paralleled the far side of the Rio Grande River. "I can see why people decided to make this place their home. The views are amazing."

"And the cliffs above made for great lodging."

They walked down the trail to one of the small cave-like alcoves bordering the path. They peered into a cozy space. Studying the room's interior, Catherine noticed that the ceiling had been blackened with soot from ancient cooking fires. Several small holes in the walls likely held racks for weaving. Along the floor were carved niches used for storing food and materials. The alcoves all faced south to provide welcome solar heat during the winter months.

A solitary picnic table in a nearby grove of pine trees provided a secluded place to sit. Once he and Catherine were settled, Steve removed sandwiches from his daypack and handed one to Catherine.

"What's so important that you need to swear me to secrecy?" Catherine asked as she started on her sandwich.

Steve visually examined the area and seeing no one within his field of view, felt confident they had sufficient privacy. For long minutes he avoided speaking. Catherine began to appreciate the sensitive nature of the issue. "I don't really know quite how to explain this, but I'll try."

He described that since it was now becoming known that certain governments had agreements and relationships with various extraterrestrial groups, Los Alamos had taken on a new role. He explained that its scope of operations had always involved highly classified matters. "Therefore, it was easy for them to take the next step."

Steve paused to take another bite from his sandwich. Catherine's mind was swirling with questions. "Which is?"

"Los Alamos does a lot more than what they tell the public." Steve spoke with a gravity that caused Catherine to tighten her breathing. "The fact is: We've been serving as a neutral zone for discussions with the ET visitors, or I should say—'extraterrestrial partners.'"

"And you are participating in these . . . discussions?"

"My superiors drafted me to head up the environmental impact committee for something that's called the Interspecies Council. We meet with multiple ET groups, technically referred to as EBEs or Extraterrestrial Biological Entities. But let's back up. Nuclear weapons are now seen as messy and obsolete compared to the weapons technology of the ET's. That realization changed the federal government's mission here rather radically. Now the emphasis is on figuring out how advanced extraterrestrial technology and those who control it might help or hinder Earth's geopolitical relationships. And of necessity, we explore how humans might best relate to a variety of other species."

"And just what is being decided?" asked Catherine carefully, fearful of the answer.

"No conclusions yet, but our main purpose is to negotiate the future of humans on Planet Earth."

Catherine stared into the distance, her mind attempting to wrap around Steve's stunning statements. She so wanted to simply forget what he had just told her.

Steve sensed that Catherine was distressed by his words. "As you can imagine, we grapple with huge issues. We talk about population control—that the planet simply cannot sustain itself under current conditions. A large reduction, either nature-generated or artificially-initiated, is a topic of much conversation. A lot of this has to do with water—freshwater has become a very valuable commodity. Certain private parties are seeking to monopolize it and price it out of the range of the poor."

"Yes, I know."

"There are many factors in the mix: underground cities; bases on the moon and Mars; and who's in control of what."

Catherine could feel an internal panic building inside her. Her automatic response was: "I've met several of the ETs, or rather, hybrids, or 'blended humans,' as some prefer to be called. They seem trustworthy . . . or at least the ones I know."

"They all have different agendas and value systems, especially regarding humans, and some of them have much more influence than others."

Catherine struggled to speak. "You seem to be saying that some kind of rating and filtering process is taking place. If you're deciding the fate of millions or billions, what happens to those who are considered expendable? If you're moving people off the planet, do you evacuate scientists, artists and teachers and leave the mafia, drug dealers, dictators and troublemakers behind? Who's wise enough to make such choices, and who has the power to do what? This is madness!"

Steve looked away. "Yes. Madness. I've aged ten years just thinking about this. But at least we're trying to make some good decisions—that's the best we can do under the circumstances." Steve was resigned and exhausted.

"It's not just about certain groups of ETs or humans," he continued, "We're also dealing with how to position the relationships between nation-states—those that will continue to exist . . . It's really complicated."

Catherine sought some form of mental consolation, forcing her panic into rational thought. "Humans are a resilient species, and we've had to adjust to major change before. Now we need to learn how to share our planet with others who have an agenda perhaps somewhat different from ours. You know, this could be a good thing—humans are not doing such a great job of it right now."

"Maybe, but consider how the arrival of Europeans impacted the indigenous cultures in Africa, Asia, and the Americas."

"Disastrous . . . But could it be different this time?"

"When I have time to think about this, I come up with two possibilities: If we could put our various differences and judgments aside, we might be able to undertake some kind of great leap forward in human consciousness. Or . . . we could all end up serving as global hospice workers."

"Likely some of both I suspect," lamented Catherine, "But what if this is like the person who finds out he or she has only a few months or years to live? Once the person gets over the shock of realizing their mortality, it often leads them to focus on what really matters."

"I think you're on to something. Maybe this is humanity's mother-of-all-wake-up-calls, telling us we'd better get our act together because our days are numbered."

"Yes, and maybe, finally, we'd realize our connectedness to not just other humans, but to other species as well—and to honor the beauty of this marvelous planet that we've been given as a stupendous gift."

"That's a great way to frame it—as a profound *opportunity* for humanity and it's multi-species partners. Whether or not it plays out this way, is of course, a big question. Still, all of this weighs heavily on me. Every day I'm thinking about how this is going to affect the children of the world. It's like I'm creating a future I won't inhabit . . . but they will. And what will it look like? What are we leaving to them? I'm not sure I'm the right person to be deciding such things."

"Well, who the hell is?" asked Catherine. She observed the tears building in Steve's eyes as he shared the weight of his personal responsibility with her.

"Come," he said. "Let's walk. I have to walk."

The two gathered up their sandwich wrappings and stepped into the warm, healing sunlight beyond the trees. How peaceful this natural world felt to Catherine. This mountainside, rich with simple archeological history, seemed so far removed from the future-shaping decisions occurring nearby. It was just too much for the average human brain to process, thought Catherine. Yet, the issues demanded attention. They would not rest.

As they walked down the trail, the pathway led into an area atop a wide stone ledge. Catherine stood on the ledge and savored the view across the Rio Grande Valley to the Sangre de Cristo Mountain Range on the valley's far side, where winter snows provided the fields below with essential water. Above the mountains, a flotilla of white clouds tumbled through a cobalt sky.

Catherine inhaled the sweet smell of sage carried her way by a soft breeze. She suspected the sage grew in the quiet meadow below her, filled with native grasses and plump juniper trees. She welcomed the sensual distraction, as her mind wanted to reject all the scary things that her dear friend had just described. She directed her attention to the landscape, richly reminiscent of a hardy people living out their lives on this spectacular, high-altitude plateau. Catherine closed her eyes in an attempt to catch a glimpse of that long-ago reality. Instead, she found herself as *the watched one*. The eyes of the future were gazing at her, asking pivotal questions that would soon decide the fate of humanity. How would the people of Planet Earth respond to the present whirlwind of challenge, complexity and change? With selfish violence, with resignation . . . or with courage, collaboration, imagination, and love?

As Catherine breathed in the crisp mountain air, the chaos in her mind yielded to the peace in her heart. And she was deeply grateful.

The far-away cry of a hawk broke the stillness. Catherine smiled. She now knew what she needed to do.

APPENDIX A

Proposed Allocation of Funding for the ACJC
(See Chapter Thirty Three)

Program Description	Amount in USD
Financial relief for two billion absolute poor	$1 trillion
World Innovation Fund for social/economic/political/technical ideas	$50 billion
Global distribution of Universal Energy power generation devices	$300 billion
Clean water and sanitation projects	$300 billion
Climate, economic and political refugee relief	$500 billion
Protection of high biodiversity and ecologically-sensitive areas	$400 billion
Support for endangered and threatened Indigenous cultures	$150 billion
Debt relief for small farmers and training in agroecology	$300 billion

Reduction of animal factory farms	$50 billion
Education of girls and women	$200 billion
Fund for independent journalism	$30 billion
Student debt relief	$1 trillion
Low income food relief and nutritional programs	$400 billion
Low income mortgage assistance	$300 billion
Global education and training	$300 billion
USA High Speed Rail	$100 billion
Implementation of Fair Trade global economic relationships	$300 billion
Infrastructure repair/rebuild/ village relocation	$800 billion
Increase Social Security payments to low-income recipients	$1.5 trillion
Environmental restoration and wildlife and oceans protection	<u>$1 trillion</u>
Sub Total	$8.780 trillion
Balance reserved for future projects	<u>$6.220 trillion</u>
TOTAL	**$15 trillion**

To successfully address the range of global problems, spending levels greater than what is commonly proposed will be required. Ignoring or minimizing the full cost of response and remediation may serve the short-term needs of policymakers, but it fails to communicate the true nature of the problem to the public at large.

The ACJC's challenge is to ensure that funds are deployed in the most transparent, fair and effective way possible. Equitable sharing of global financial resources would trigger an explosion of individual and collective creativity, while also contributing to a heightened sense of individual and community security. Improved security could go a long way toward reducing the pressure for armed conflict and wholesale migration. Increased global financial aid could also provide a range of powerful, quality-of-life improvement opportunities for marginalized populations.

During subsequent discussions at the ACJC, a series of key action steps were proposed:

- Create a Universal Energy training program. The program would enable participants to establish Universal Energy Design, Build and Operate Centers around the world, which would, in turn, accelerate the global deployment of the new energy technology and rapidly reduce CO_2 emissions.

- Establish a special fund to assist Third-World populations threatened by the impacts of climate change. Create a collaborative of expertise to provide the necessary leadership and technical knowledge to enable relocation if required.

- Allocate funds for biodiversity protection and recovery and purchase land slated for development near environmentally sensitive areas. Once the land is acquired, it would be transferred to land conservation and wildlife protection organizations.

- Provide universal family planning education for women and men, as well as abundant and free birth control information and options.

- Move quickly to reduce and eliminate the use of chemicals and pesticides on farmlands. Phase out chemically-based agriculture in favor of small- and large-scale organic agriculture. Of particular concern is the need to reduce and eventually eliminate CAFOs (Confined Animal Feeding Operations).

- Given the dire state of the oceans, immediately initiate major remedial actions to address decimation of fisheries, increasing acidification and rise in ocean temperature. Provide funding for removal of plastics and toxic materials from the seas.

- Create the World Innovation Fund, whose mission is to generate project ideas to enable people to live with greater dignity and less suffering. Educational programs would explore how our personal choices impact our direction and identity as a species.

- Remove trade barriers and international policies that disadvantage local production of goods and services. Promote Fair Trade relationships that encourage sustainable, environmentally-sound practices, and provide local people with a fair wage and safe working conditions.

- Bolster programs to support Indigenous cultures, with an emphasis on the need to reach out to Native People struggling with poverty, racism, and toxic industrial development.

- Offer a wide variety of creative ideas for utilizing digital communications to improve women's lives through online education, healthcare and economic and financial training. Create curricula that would enable women to explore digital media as a means for self-empowerment.

- Explore how global economic policy often promotes insecurity and uncertainty by design. Examine how domination and power-over has become the prevailing force in the world and how it can exacerbate world problems and obstruct practical solutions.

APPENDIX B

What Makes Water Special?

What is it about water that makes it so special? Over forty anomalies testify to its uniqueness. These anomalies include unusually high melting and boiling points and high liquid surface tension. Water also boasts a high heat of vaporization and fusion (amount of heat needed to melt ice). Unlike most liquids, water's weight decreases when becoming a solid. Water reaches its most dense state at +4°C or 39.2°F. If water *increased* its weight when solid, ice would sink, freezing lakes and streams into a solid block.

Fortunately, water has a high specific heat factor. Thus, it's an excellent temperature moderator. Given the fact that all life-forms are made up mostly of water, this characteristic is essential for supporting life. And water's efficacy as a universal solvent is unmatched. Water is the ideal liquid for cooking our foods, manufacturing our products and cleaning up our messes.

When we ingest water, the biological, chemical and other components in water are transferred to our cells and serve either to support or harm our internal bacteria. Not surprisingly, the health of our internal bacteria strongly determines our overall physical and mental health.

A healthy environment is necessary to support biological life. Thus, the quality of care and treatment we render to our sources of water has everything to do with the ability of water-dependent life-forms to continue to exist.

"Water's Experience"

When we drink water, the biological, chemical and other components contained in water are carried throughout our cells. This includes "water's experience" as it makes it way from its source. In today's reality, water finds itself subjected to ever-present and increasing levels of pollution and miles of straight and often deteriorating piping. This "experience" tends to rob water of its original physical structure acquired by flowing through rocky, curving watercourses and waterfalls. When water is highly processed, such as in the case with distillation or reverse osmosis, it loses much or all of its health-enhancing properties. When subjected to such conditions, water will seek to "become whole," to recover its lost qualities by drawing its missing chemical components from its immediate environment. Thus, it's important to avoid relying on highly processed types of drinking water that do not exist in nature.

In nature, water runs free. It flows and swirls, creating multiple vortices and is bathed in abundant sunlight, minerals and free oxygen. Good, clean, vitalized and properly "structured" water is essential to maintaining an optimum level of human and environmental health.

ACKNOWLEDGEMENTS

Where to start? So many great researchers, innovators, inventors, writers and speakers have contributed to this story. On the technology side, I was curious about the long-term purpose of the so-called Deep Underground Military Bases, commonly labeled D.U.M.B., of which at least 120 exist in the U.S., distributed under major cities. Some are over a mile deep and connected to networks of tunnels. Many other countries have their own underground facilities as well. For example: Sweden has placed an entire naval base inside a mountain. But are there others of a non-military nature? If so, what is their purpose, why are they kept so secret, and who besides the military are building and populating them? Thanks to the Internet for providing information on the subject.

Then there's the incredibly courageous, profoundly disturbing and meticulous research undertaken by Sterling and Peggy Seagrave to expose one of the great state secrets of the Twentieth Century—the fate of the Japanese and Nazi treasures recovered by Allied agents following WWII. Their seminal book, *Gold Warriors*, provided me with a key plot concept. But what happened to all those vast caches of gold and booty? To answer that question, I've drawn upon the financial sleuthing of Catherine Austin Fitts (Solari Report) and Dr. Joseph Farrell. They have convincingly documented the tens of trillions of squirreled away in a parallel financial system replete with multi-trillion-dollar, black military and private "special compartmented" budgets and hidden offshore bank accounts. It is their conclusion that this covert monetary system funds the growing security state and provides the financing for an assortment of advanced technologies, multi-decade-long secret space program, and sci-fi weapons systems completely unknown to the general public. Likewise, I've learned much from Foster and Kimberly Gamble's efforts to educate the public through the *THRIVE Community* network regarding the corrosive effect on our world resulting from the excessive concentration of wealth. The Gamble's admonition to "follow the money" clearly exposes the true agenda of forces that would manipulate society in highly deleterious ways.

Richard Dolan, a powerful voice exposing un-disclosures, has served as core inspiration to me in developing the framework for fleshing out the two fundamental concepts that could change the world as we know it—in a positive way. One: Provide the world with an energy source that cannot be controlled by an oligarchic elite, and two: Redistribute the ill-gotten financial riches of the planet from the few to the many to create a more equitable, prosperous and stable world.

On the water side, the pioneering water master and Austrian naturalist is Viktor Schauberger. His elucidating work with water revealed to anyone who would listen the vast potential of water's natural energy. His biography, *Living Water*, served as my introduction to this utterly fascinating and portentous subject. Equally revolutionary in regards to water's secret life is the work of Masaru Emoto. His book, *The Hidden Messages of Water*, presented to the world the possibility that water has memory and history—that water holds all the knowledge and experience it has acquired when exposed to various stimuli, including people's emotions. What a concept! What does this tell us about how we treat water? Or how we *should* treat water.

And a note of appreciation goes to Will Allen of Growing Power, Venice Williams of Alice's Garden, the Victory Garden Initiative whose motto is "Move Grass. Grow Food", and the many other passionate Milwaukee folks striving to create wonderful community gardens and more self-reliant urban habitats. Their powerful examples demonstrate that good, healthy food can be grown in urban settings year-round.

I was impressed by the work of the Milwaukee Water Commons to bring more public attention to the precious nature of water. In terms of treating water as a sacred, life-giving substance, I needed to look no further than the tradition of "Water Walks" and what it means to be a "Water Woman" in the Native American Ojibwe tradition. The *Nibi* (Water) Walks are Indigenous-led, extended ceremonies to pray for the water. Many Native American women of the Upper Midwest region have walked their way, undeterred by rain, cold, snow and heat, around each of the Great Lakes and other major bodies of surface water. As they walk they remember that, "Every step is taken in prayer and gratitude for water, our life giving force."

A great archive of water-related publications exist, but one that woke me up to the unfathomable suffering that several billion impoverished people around the world have been and are facing due to the scarcity and unhealthy quality of water is *The Price of Thirst*, by Karen Piper. Her expose of the duplicity and greed surrounding efforts to privatize global water supplies I found astonishing in terms of its toll of human suffering and considerable threat to the fragile balance of the world's interrelated water systems. This is something we should all be very concerned about.

I give thanks to my life-partner Kate for sharing her knowledge of human psychology, which immeasurably improved the quality of the story and the depth of the characters. I extend to her my deepest gratitude and heart-felt appreciation.

And finally, a gracious bow of the head to the Great Water Mystery, herself, for the daily gift of life.

ABOUT THE AUTHOR

Charles Bensinger is a visionary, educator, and writer. His curiosity about life, history, science, the human condition and its potential for the extraordinary, has led him to author ten published books. His subjects of focus have included: emerging media technologies, archeology, mythology, popular culture, politics, biology, evolution, spirituality and speculative fiction.

Most recently, deep concern over the global climate change crisis has compelled him to create the **People of the Change Trilogy**. This exciting and timely epic adventure takes us way beyond traditional thinking and offers potent solutions to address humanity's greatest challenge. Charles appreciates the changing moods of Lake Michigan, and visits the lakeshore in Milwaukee, Wisconsin nearly every day.

RELEVANT RESOURCES

For websites, books, papers, videos, conferences:
www.peopleofthechange.com

Subjects referenced:

- Underground military bases
- Breakaway civilization
- Secret Space Program and hidden system of finance
- Recovery of Axis loot following WWII
- Water protection and education groups
- Indigenous-led Water Walks
- Water's memory and restoring water's "liveness"
- The THRIVE Movement
- Various climate change activist organizations
- Amazing water research and water phenomena videos

The **People of the Change Trilogy** provides powerful and original solutions to the food, energy and water crises that threaten to plunge humanity into a death spiral. The purpose of this trilogy is to offer a bold, new vision for the future of all life on Planet Earth.

Other books in the People of the Change Trilogy
Radical Option, Book One (2014)
Beyond Fire, Book Two (2015)

**For information and discussion regarding the
ideas and issues put forth in this book, visit:**

www.peopleofthechange.com

Made in the USA
Charleston, SC
01 December 2016